Copyright 2012

Also from the author

The Captive Series

Captured (Book 1) ✓

Renegade (Book 2) ✓

Refugee (Book 3) ✓

Salvation (Book 4) ✓

The Kindred Series

Kindred (Book 1)

Ashes (Book 2)

Kindled (Book 3)

Inferno (Book 4)

Phoenix Rising (Book 5)

The Ravening Series

Ravenous (Book 1) ✓

Taken Over (Book 2) ✓

Reclamation (Book 3)

The Survivor Chronicles:

Book 1, The Upheaval

Book 2, The Divide

CHAPTER 1

I turned the rifle over in my hands, rotating it slowly back and forth as I stared out at the dimly lit field. Not even the crickets were chirping in the still summer night, but then it had been strangely hushed ever since The Freezing had occurred. I tried to convince myself that I would become used to it one day, but it hadn't happened yet, and I knew I was just lying to myself.

There was no way to become accustomed to the lack of noise in a world that had once been alive and thriving with it. To do so would mean that I was ok with the reason behind the quiet. And I was not, nor would I *ever* be ok with the death and mayhem that the aliens had unleashed upon Planet Earth. I would never be able to accept the horror and loss that had been inflicted upon all of us because of them. They had taken my mother, and they had taken Cade.

My mind shied away from the memory of our last moment together, when he had cut the rope that had been joining us, sacrificing himself for me. He loved me. He'd told me that just seconds before he'd been taken, but I still didn't understand why he'd done it. My life wasn't worth his. It certainly wasn't worth much since he'd been taken from me.

I closed my eyes and took a deep breath as I tried to ease the anguish constricting my chest. Even without him I wanted to amount to something, to be a better, stronger, person, but I was choked by my grief, drowning within it and I didn't know how to swim. Not anymore. I'd kept afloat through my father's death, I'd had no choice but to continue on after my mother's, and though I was still breathing and still moving, I was acutely aware of the fact that I was no longer able to *live* without Cade. I was a hollow shell of the person I'd once been, and that person hadn't been that great to begin with. I simply couldn't seem to recoup after this loss, simply couldn't put myself back together again. It was more fight than I had left in me anymore, unless of course I was killing something. I had plenty of fight and anger within me for that.

I was ready for a fight but the alien monsters had been strangely scarce for the past couple of days. I didn't know what that meant, but I did know that I wasn't going to quit hunting and killing them. Not until I knew for certain if Cade was alive or not.

If there was any chance he was still alive, I was going to do *everything* I could to get him back.

I leaned forward, my hand tensed on the gun as I stopped switching it back and forth. "Do you see something?"

Bret sat up beside me, his broad shoulder brushed against mine. I didn't have to look at him to know the tender warmth of his soft green eyes, or the gentle sweep of his dirty blond hair. His handsome face was beloved to me. Until Cade had reappeared in my life, and shown me what it was to *fall* in love with someone, I may very well have married Bret and built a simple life with him. But then I had come to know Cade again, and everything had changed. I loved Bret, I truly did, but Cade owned my heart and soul, he owned every bit of me. He always would.

It saddened me that Bret had been hurt by what had happened between Cade and I, and that he still held out hope that we would one day be together again, no matter how much I tried to make him understand that we wouldn't. Bret wanted to believe my feelings for Cade had developed because Cade had saved my life, and because I'd been traumatized by the loss of my mother. He had chosen to believe that one day I would become as convinced as the rest of them that Cade was dead, and that I would turn to him again.

However, even if Cade really was dead, a fact I refused to believe, I wouldn't turn to Bret again. I couldn't. The mere thought of Cade being gone for good was nearly enough to crush me, but if it were ever confirmed I didn't know how I would react, how I would handle it. I didn't know if I would be much good as a human being anymore, not that I was all that great right now, but I was terrified I'd become even worse.

There could never be anyone else, and I would never do that to Bret. He deserved far better than the cold, deadened person that I had become. Far better than the shattered being I would be if Cade was lost forever. Bret deserved to be loved; he deserved the kind of intense wonder and joy I had found with Cade, even if it had only been for a brief time.

I just wished Bret would finally see that.

"No," I murmured.

"It's almost time to head back anyway."

My fingers tapped on the gun. I wasn't ready to go back.

It was a patrol, just like this one, that had been unable to save Cade's life, but had saved mine. Though I might not feel like my life was worth much right now, there were others out there that may need our help. They could appear at any time, just as the seven of us had appeared on the beach out of nowhere.

I rose and stretched the taut muscles in my back and legs. Swinging the rifle over my shoulder, I bent to grab the flashlight off the ground. My entire body ached from being immobile for so long; I had to move around a bit to get the blood flowing back into my feet.

Bret grabbed hold of my arm; I froze as he placed a finger against my mouth. Still half bent over, my eyes went back to the field near where we had been sitting. We were on the outskirts, surrounded by trees, but I felt incredibly vulnerable all of a sudden.

My eyes narrowed as I searched for whatever it was that had caught Bret's attention. Then, across the field, I saw a flicker of movement. I quickly folded back onto the ground, trying to make myself as invisible as possible as all of my senses kicked into hyper drive. It had been days since we'd last seen any hint of the aliens, but now there was something out there, on the edge of the high grass.

I sensed motion to my right, but it wasn't aliens over there. Instead, it was the others from our group. I caught a brief glimpse of Darnell creeping through the underbrush to get a closer look, his dark skin and camo fatigues nearly blended in with the night surrounding him. Sgt. Darnell Hastings held the highest military rank, and was in charge of the five remaining soldiers left in our group of survivors. One had been killed, and the other one had split off toward Rhode Island in search of his sister and nieces. I hoped he had made it, but we would never know for sure.

Darnell had taken charge of training the survivors, or at least the ones who were eager to learn how to shoot, fight, and defend ourselves. The thing I would like most right now was to fight, to kill, and to destroy every single one of the things that had ruined all of our lives. My heart thumped with eager anticipation of what was to come. I was anxious for blood and retribution.

Darnell motioned for us to stay where we were. We'd been under his strict training for the past two weeks, but he still didn't think we were capable of much. I chafed at the constraints he placed on us, I wanted this. I *needed* this.

Darnell continued to creep forward; he made some signal to Lloyd and Sarah to follow close behind. The three of them had been stationed together for nearly two years before The Freezing; they knew each other's movements, gestures, and thoughts without even having to speak. It was fascinating to watch them move and work together in near unison.

Though the aliens had disbanded all branches of the military seven months after their arrival, these three had lived within the Wareham, Buzzards Bay area. Every day they had met up with twenty three other members of the military from the area to continue their training in secret. Thankfully they had been as doubtful about the alien's proclamation of peace as I'd been.

They were lucky enough to have been together when The Freezing occurred; eight of them had survived it. None of them had been able to get back to their families or find them again. They sought revenge and justice just as badly as I did, and I trusted them to one day make me as finely honed a killing machine as they were. They crept to the edge of the trees, staying low to the ground as they took up new positions closer to the field.

I chewed on my bottom lip as I brought my rifle back around and clasped it before me. I was tempted to move a little closer but remained where I was. I wasn't a soldier under his command, but I listened to Darnell. He knew what he was doing, I was still inept. I wanted him to teach me everything he knew and pissing him off by disobeying him wasn't going to help with that.

Thanks to Darnell, and the situation we had been tossed into, I could handle a gun with far more competency than I could have a couple of weeks ago. I hadn't been good at firing a gun in the beginning, but lately I seemed to have acquired some strange natural ability for it. We didn't get to practice often, as we couldn't waste the ammo or draw attention to ourselves, but the few times I'd been able to fire a gun recently, I hadn't missed.

From my hidden position in the tall grass, I focused my attention on the thing moving across the field directly in front of me. I couldn't quite determine what it was yet, but it didn't appear to be one of the massive tick/octopus/crab/jellyfish looking things that had been able to reawaken the frozen people by violently draining their blood from them. People we still couldn't figure out how to reawaken on our own. People that we weren't even sure were still alive anymore, or if we would *ever* be able to save them. So much time had passed since The Freezing that it seemed impossible that any of them could still be alive within their frozen forms.

However, none of us were willing to give up hope yet.

If this was an alien creature, then it was much smaller than those we'd seen up until now. They were usually large and bloated like a tick full of the blood of humans. The aliens themselves were exceptionally human in appearance with their dark hair, eyes, and olive skinned to darker hued complexions. They had rarely come to earth from their spaceships before The Freezing, and there was no sign that they had returned since the attack had started.

I doubted they would. They wanted our lives and our blood, but they had never really shown much interest in our planet. I rested my hand against the rough bark of a white oak as I strained to see across the field. I couldn't see what was causing the movement, but if the motion of the grass was any indication, it was getting closer.

The hair on the nape of my neck stood on end as a cold sweat began to trickle down my back. Then, the grass parted and a young girl stepped out. My jaw dropped, my hand clenched on the trunk of the tree. I don't think I would have been anymore flabbergasted to see Elvis himself stepping out of the field.

I didn't know where she had come from, but there was something so lost and forlorn about her that I had the strangest urge to cry. One strap dangled against the front of her blood stained sundress. Hair the color of copper hung over her thin, delicate shoulders. More blood streaked her forehead and cheeks, and her eyes were hollow in her thin, pale face. She was so small, so delicate and fragile that my heart ached for her, she reminded me so much of Abby that I nearly burst from the woods and ran to her. I managed to stop myself only because of the fact that Bret had partially stepped in front of me.

Darnell gestured to Sarah, one of his soldiers, and then pointed toward the young girl who was staring unseeingly at the woods. Sarah nodded before slipping into the shadows. I knew which way she had gone, but I lost sight of her almost immediately. When she reappeared it was from three hundred feet away on our right, and she was moving out of the woods toward the little girl's location.

The girl turned toward her, but otherwise didn't acknowledge the fact that Sarah was even there. *She has to be in shock*, I thought crazily. The fact that Sarah had a gun trained on her probably wasn't helping, but I would have done the same thing. If there was one thing we had learned recently it was that anyone and anything could be dangerous, and to *never* let our guards down.

Sarah moved steadily toward the girl, her face remained impassive, but I could sense her confusion and hesitance. Bret grabbed hold of my arm as I made a move to get closer. I almost protested his controlling gesture, but I remained mute. I was too afraid to make any kind of noise or motion with Sarah so exposed.

"Are you ok?" Sarah demanded. The girl remained soundless and unmoving. "Can you hear me? Are you ok?"

I wasn't breathing anymore; my lungs were beginning to burn but I still couldn't bring myself to breathe. Something was wrong, this wasn't normal. Darnell seemed to sense the same thing as he rose to his feet and leveled his rifle against his shoulder.

Then it happened. It was so fast that none of us had a chance to fire a shot. One second the girl was standing there and the next she was on top of Sarah. At first I didn't understand what had happened, or who had moved first, but then it all became painfully, clearly obvious. That girl was *not* a girl.

Something lashed out of her mouth as she launched herself forward. The tentacle thing/tongue slammed into Sarah's face with a sickening crack of bone that echoed loudly throughout the still night. I couldn't move, couldn't react as Sarah's face caved in as easily as a rotten pumpkin.

That thing, which I now recognized as being eerily similar to the tentacles that came from the larger monsters that hunted us, slid down Sarah's throat as the hideous girl knocked her to the ground with far more force than I would have expected from her small frame.

By the time Darnell recovered enough to open fire on the horrific creature, it was already too late for Sarah. The creature/girl bucked as the bullets tore through her flesh. A strange hissing scream erupted from the tiny monster as it fell back. Its tentacles lashed through the air before recoiling swiftly into its mouth.

Before us, the girl/thing seemed to melt. Flesh and bone reshaped into something far different, and yet strangely familiar as one of the ugly, deadly creatures we were more familiar with unfolded from what had once been the body of a young girl.

It was not as massive as some of the others we had encountered, but this one seemed even more menacing than any of the far larger ones. For one thing, it seemed to be able to mimic a human being pretty damn *freaking* well. That was a trait that *none* of us had experienced before.

I didn't realize I was pulling the trigger until I felt the recoil of the gun in my hands. I pulled the trigger over and over again and continued to do so even after the gun was empty. The reasonable, still somewhat sane part of my mind, realized that I should stop shooting. However, I couldn't bring myself to lower the empty gun until Bret grabbed hold of it and forcefully pushed it down.

I was ashamed by the shaking that rattled my entire body causing even my teeth to chatter. I had lost my mother, I had lost Cade, I had seen far more of these things than I cared to recall, but for some strange reason I was shaking so bad I could barely stand. What I had just witnessed had rattled me so much I thought I might actually piss my pants.

It had looked so *human,* so eerily childlike, and what it had done... Well what it had done was pulverize Sarah's pretty face. Even from my distant position I could see there was nothing left to her. Tears choked me as I realized that Sarah's own mother, if she had still been alive, wouldn't have been able to recognize the smashed pile of flesh and bone before us.

"It's ok Bethy." Bret's voice trembled as he spoke the words. I wondered briefly if he believed them. I didn't. "It's ok."

I swallowed heavily, I wanted to sit but I couldn't. I had to stay strong; I couldn't let them see how disturbed I was by what had just happened. "No," I disagreed. "It's not. It hasn't been in a long time, and it never will be again."

It was the first time I'd ever expressed that thought out loud. The first time I had truly acknowledged my own growing doubts to anyone else. As I met Bret's clear green eyes I realized that the worst part was that ever optimistic and loving Bret believed it too.

CHAPTER 2

Darnell nudged the edge of the dead alien monster with the toe of his boot. The planes of his narrow face were even more defined due to the harsh compression of his full lips. He was still wearing the jacket of his camo fatigues, but it was the only thing that marked him as the soldier he had once been. His brown eyes raked over all of us before focusing on the strange creature again.

The girl the thing had pretended to be was completely gone. It was almost the color of a jellyfish except for the blood it had managed to suck out of Sarah before dying. I couldn't bring myself to look at Sarah's ruined face again. She had been a pretty woman with a quirky smile and hazel eyes but that was all gone now.

The tentacle flopped uselessly to the side as Darnell shoved it with his foot again and dropped it. "We should get going," Darnell said. "Private Price give me a hand with the body."

Private Lloyd Price looked just as shaken and horrified as I felt. His smattering of reddish freckles was stark against the pallor of his drained skin. His clear blue eyes were wide and rolling behind his glasses, his nearly orange hair was going in a thousand different directions. He wasn't much older than me, nineteen, twenty at most. He became even paler at the command. I had the distinct impression that this was not what the young private had signed up for when he enlisted. I didn't blame him in the least. I didn't like the idea of leaving Sarah here but if Darnell had asked me to help him I probably would have thrown up.

"How did it do that?" I blurted. Darnell's chocolate colored eyes slid toward me; there was no answer in his remorseless gaze. My heart was hammering, my palms were sweating; I couldn't believe I was about to say what I was going to say. "We should bring it back with us."

"Are you crazy?" Bret demanded.

I held Darnell's gaze, not at all comforted by the growing admiration for me I saw blooming in his eyes. The last thing I wanted was to touch either one of the bodies, but we couldn't leave Sarah behind, and this was the first opportunity we'd had to study one of these creatures. Dr. Bishop would be pissed if we didn't bring it back so he could examine it.

I glanced between the two broken bodies, but I couldn't bring myself to go to Sarah. She'd been a good person, and now she was gone. Though the thought of touching the creature before me was repugnant, I simply could *not* touch Sarah.

Bending down I took hold of the alien carcass lying in the grass at my feet. I had expected it to be slimy or mushy; I was surprised that it was neither. There was something about it that reminded me of silver, hard and cold when cooled, yet liquid and pliable when heated. I was so caught up in that realization that I hadn't noticed Bret had also grabbed hold of the creature until he nudged me.

"Come on Bethy let's get out of here."

I swallowed heavily and managed a small nod. Though this creature was nowhere near as large as some of the others I had seen, it was still exceptionally difficult to maneuver through the woods with its bulky weight, flopping tentacle, and insect like legs. My legs burned from exertion as we labored to slip through the trees as quietly as possible.

Before this war with the aliens I'd been reasonably fit, but I certainly wouldn't have been able to handle hauling this thing through the woods. Then again, there were many things that I wouldn't have been able to handle before, but could now. Like a gun or scuba gear or even walking over this rough terrain carrying at least a hundred pounds of monster. My legs were tired, but I wasn't sweating overly much, and my breathing wasn't labored, or at least not yet anyway.

At the top of a crest, the large boat warehouse we had discovered a week ago came into view. When I had first been rescued by the ragtag group of survivors, they had been holed up in a lobster warehouse, but that had been three housings ago. We didn't have homes anymore; we just had buildings that sheltered us until it was time to move on. Time to head into areas that the aliens had already cleared of The Frozen Ones, to move further away from the dangerous zones, though I doubted there were any safe zones out there. Not anymore.

I hated moving further away from the last place I had seen Cade, but I knew location had no meaning in my attempt to find him. For all I knew, he might not even be on this planet anymore, let alone still in the Cape Cod area. It was foolish of me to resent moving further inland, but I couldn't stop the feeling.

I resented being forced out of the only home I had ever known, the only *place* I had ever known. I didn't kid myself into thinking that I would ever have a home again, that anything would ever be the same, but I wasn't ready to let it all go either. I was like a stubborn child clinging to my pacifier, unwilling to relinquish it even though it was time. Everything I had ever known was gone, it was time to move on, but I was having a difficult time doing so.

There was no way to stop what had happened, at least not one that any of us could think of, and to stay in one place was to die. All we could hope for was to survive every day and to keep hold of the few loved ones we had left. I was more fortunate then most to still have Bret, and my brother and sister. There were others that still had family with them, but not many.

I sighed as we moved cautiously down the hill. The only good thing about all the moving was that Dr. Bishop had to leave behind all of the frozen bodies he'd collected. He still had one, but the roomful of unmoving people had been abandoned in the lobster warehouse. I thought I should feel more guilt over that decision, but I found there was little room for emotion, or compassion, within me anymore. Those things had to be suspended in this new and deadly world, they would eat me alive if I dwelt on them too much.

There had been nothing that we could do for those people; Dr. Bishop had tried everything he could think of to reawaken them from their frozen state. Nothing had worked. I'd disliked leaving them behind, I wasn't completely dead inside, but if we were to survive then the deadweight had to be dropped. I couldn't dwell on those decisions, not if I planned to keep my sanity anyway. We hadn't happily abandoned The Frozen Ones, we had simply moved on because we had to survive.

Survival was the number one concern now. It was what drove us all.

As we approached the warehouse a few people emerged from the shadows. Their guns were at the ready as they prepared to defend the people within if necessary. More emerged as it became clear who we were, and what we carried with us. Silence came over the group as we slipped into the shadows of the cavernous building.

Most of the people were asleep, scattered about on makeshift beds. The dim illumination of the lamps flickered over the room and cast shadows over the windowless metal walls. There had originally been sixty people within the group when they first discovered us; there were only thirty or so left. Some had gone out on their own, some had refused to move on, and others had been killed.

I spotted my younger sister, Abby, as she made her way toward us. She moved with easy grace through the people sprawled on the floor. Her resemblance to our mother never failed to amaze me, from her long coffee hair, to her gleaming chocolate eyes and petite stature. Our mother may be gone, but there was no denying that she lived on in Abby.

She was almost to us when she stopped and her hand flew to her mouth. She fixated on the thing between Bret and I. "What happened!?" she cried.

"Long story," I muttered as I searched for some place to put our load down.

"Are you ok?"

I managed a nod, but I knew she didn't buy it. Who could with what we held between us? "Where's Bishop?" Bret inquired.

"Where else would he be?" Abby retorted.

Bret and I carried the thing toward one of the back rooms. Dr. Bishop set up a laboratory and medical area in every new place that we moved into. Before The Freezing his main area of interest had been research; unfortunately after The Freezing conducting research on me had become his main area of interest. In the few weeks I'd known him I'd been stuck with more needles than in my entire seventeen years. If I'd been a dog I probably would have bit him by now, but I'd actually come to like Bishop, needles and all.

The doctor appeared in the doorway of his newest laboratory area. Even in the dim light I could clearly see the excitement that filled his gaze as he stared at the thing we held. "You're a strange man," I informed him as we moved past. "Where would you like this thing?"

He hurried in behind us, a new spring in his step. He shoved papers off a counter that had been used for equipment repairs before the aliens had left all sense of a normal life nonexistent. "Up here! Up here!" he said excitedly before flitting away.

Bret rolled his eyes and shook his head. I had grown to like the seemingly frantic and discombobulated doctor, but most still found him a little creepy and a bit annoying. Bret also didn't like the extra attention that Bishop focused on me, even if it was only because I was his favorite pin cushion.

I dropped the thing on the counter, grateful to be rid of the weight of the hideous creature. I walked over to the sink to wash my hands and arms in the large metal basin. I scrubbed vigorously, using the small scrub brush to clean the blood from under my nails. "This is amazing! Amazing!" Bishop muttered excitedly. "Maybe we can find a live specimen."

I shot him a look, while Bret gaped at him. "Count your blessings with this one doc," I informed him.

Bishop wasn't listening to me though. His gray eyes were narrowed in concentration behind his glasses as he bent close to the thing. It appeared that I had been replaced as Bishop's favorite thing to poke at, for the time being.

"It's true." I hadn't heard my older brother Aiden approach, but there he was in the doorway.

"Yes, yes," Bishop said quickly. "We are very lucky. Lucky indeed."

Aiden's mahogany eyes fixated on the creature lying on the counter. He had become the doc's assistant, eager to explore and learn anything that Bishop was willing to teach him. Before the aliens arrived a year ago Aiden had aspired to be a doctor, a scientist, or perhaps even work for NASA. He had yearned to know the secrets the skies held. Unfortunately we knew the answers to those secrets now, and they hadn't been as fantastic as Aiden, or any of us, had dreamed. After the aliens arrived our education had become more restricted and NASA had been shut down six months later. Aiden may have lost his dreams, but his curiosity had never waned. He was eagerly turning that inquisitiveness and intelligence to research and medical training with Bishop.

"Awesome," Aiden breathed.

I shook my head at my brother as he hurried forward. We were blood, good friends and I loved him deeply, but he confounded me. Abby must have woken him as his honey blond hair, so similar to mine, was disheveled and standing on end. Though both of my siblings had brown eyes, mine were the color of a glimmering amethyst, like my father's had been. Both Abby and Aiden had freckles speckling their noses, but my freckles were more prominent as they spread over my cheeks, especially now with all the time I'd been spending outside.

His eyes were still swollen with sleep but he was alert as he eyed the creature like it was a pot of gold.

"You wouldn't think it was so awesome if you'd seen what it did to Sarah," I told him.

His face went slack as he turned back to me. "Sarah's dead?"

"Yes."

Regret flashed across his handsome features, he looked slightly abashed as his fair skin colored. "What did it do?" Bishop asked quietly and for the first time without excitement.

It was Bret that filled them in on the awful events as I couldn't find the words to describe the atrocity. I didn't think there were any. I leaned against the wall, staring at my ratty shoes as I fought the urge to vomit. Darnell joined us in the room, his upper lip curled as he stopped before the metal counter. I didn't know where they had placed Sarah until she could be buried, and I didn't want to know. I'd seen enough of the damage that had been done to her.

"Amazing," Bishop murmured when Bret finished filling him in on the details.

"Stop saying that!" My tone was far more piercing than I'd meant for it to be, but my fear and irritation came surging to the forefront. "They're *not* amazing. They're awful Bishop, they're *awful*."

They all stared at me like I was a talking penguin. I'd been so emotionless lately that any sign of feeling was a surprising to them. Relief flickered over Aiden's features and Bret's shoulders slouched.

"You're right," Bishop conceded.

"What do you say we get some sleep and let the science wizards do their thing?" Bret touched my arm gently.

The sympathy in his gaze set my teeth on edge but I simply nodded my agreement because I was too exhausted to really care about it right now. I had to get away from that *thing* for awhile. All I desired was to lie down for a little bit before we had to do it all over again tomorrow. Abby was sitting on a pile of blankets in the corner of the building that we had claimed as our own. The glow of the small lamp highlighted the anxiety marring her delicate features. Jenna was next to her, curled up on her side as she slept soundly.

"That thing really is dead, right?" Abby asked anxiously.

"It's dead," Bret confirmed.

I curled up on my own thin pile of blankets and tucked an old sweatshirt under my head. Facing the wall, I turned my back on the others. I didn't want them to see the agony and defeat that was steadily crushing my soul. I stared ahead unseeingly as the others settled in around me. I hated the night the most, when I was alone, when I was stuck with just my thoughts and my loss. When I was trapped with the realization that I may never see Cade again, never touch him, never kiss him, never have the chance to tell him that I loved him too.

I'd always held out some hope that I would find him, held out some hope that one day we would be reunited. It was that hope that had kept me going for the past couple of weeks, but after what I'd seen tonight, nearly all of that hope had deflated like a popped balloon.

How could we defeat these things, how would I ever get Cade back from them even if I did miraculously find him alive? They were everywhere, they were far more powerful than us, and now they had revealed that their *monsters* could even look like us, not just them.

For the first time I let myself accept the fact that I couldn't, that I probably wouldn't find him. I curled up in a tighter ball as I pressed my fist against my mouth. I bit on my knuckles in order to keep my screams and sobs suppressed. I couldn't breathe, could barely see, and I wasn't sure I could survive this bone wrenching anguish but though tears burned my eyes, I didn't shed them.

Cade had once told me that he was the only person I trusted enough to fall apart in front of, and he was right. When he'd been with me he'd made me strong enough to allow myself to let go of my rigid self control. I'd trusted him enough to let him see my weakness, my cowardice, my inner self, and he had loved me for it anyway. He had stripped my soul bare, had made me fall in love with him, and he had *left* me. He'd sacrificed himself for me when I would have preferred that he hadn't. He'd left me in this hideous world, one that I was tired of, one that I hated. If it wasn't for my siblings I wasn't sure I would continue on, that I would keep fighting. There wasn't much left to fight for.

I hated my thoughts, hated the weakness they revealed about myself. Most people would choose to keep fighting, everyone else in this building did, but I was a coward; I was weak, broken, and barely able to breathe throughout the increasingly lengthy days and nights. Everyone around me was a fighter, a survivor. I was proud of them all. That pride didn't extend to me. I wouldn't leave my siblings, but it was a constant battle to go on *for* them.

If something ever happened to them...

No, it couldn't. It simply couldn't. I wasn't strong enough to survive that too.

I could only focus on surviving the loss of Cade now. I would not fall apart, I would not cry. I would not give into my weakness, not now, not ever again. There was no point in crying. I still had Abby, Aiden, Bret, Molly, and as much as Jenna and I didn't always get along, she was a part of our group. She was a connection to a past life forever lost to us all.

    I would not fall apart. I had suffered losses before. I had watched my father die; my mother had been taken during The Freezing. I would endure this, I would continue to breathe, I would continue to walk, and I would continue to eat. I would wake up every day, and I would go to sleep every night, and I would continue to go on living without Cade, even though I was dead inside.

CHAPTER 3

"Did you get any sleep?"

I blinked blearily at Bishop as he stuck a piece of cotton against my skin and turned to grab a band-aid. "Some," I lied.

I pat the band-aid into place as I slid off the makeshift table. He eyed me carefully, his gray eyes red rimmed behind his glasses. He couldn't say much to me as it was apparent that he hadn't gotten any sleep either. The creature was still on the counter, splayed out like the specimen it was. Bishop and Aiden had already gathered samples, and had begun to dissect and study the monster. I eyed it warily; I was half convinced that it was going to come back to life at any moment. I pulled the gun I had placed on the counter a little closer to me.

"Why do you keep taking samples of my blood? It hasn't done you any good yet."

Bishop shrugged absently as he placed the syringe full of blood into a test tube. "Maybe one day I'll get access to some real equipment and I'll be able to run some real tests. Until then, maybe something will come up."

"Or maybe you'll discover someone else with a blood type other than O."

He gave me a wry smile, but I knew he didn't believe that. He was set in his belief that my blood held the key to helping the frozen people, convinced that because my blood type was different than the other survivors I was somehow unique. Everyone else that had survived The Freezing, or at least the ones Bishop had encountered were all type O, I was not.

I thought he was wrong, but I was willing to give him my blood just in case he wasn't. There may be no hope for my mom and Cade, but there were other families out there that needed it.

"And if you don't find the answers?" I asked.

I was immediately sorry I'd asked the question. His forehead furrowed in confusion, his dove gray eyes darkened with worry. It was obvious that such a thought had never even occurred to him. Bishop had never once considered the possibility that he wouldn't find the equipment he needed, or the answers he sought. I admired his dogged determination and optimism; I leaned more toward pessimism. I wasn't sure if I'd always been that way, or if surviving the car accident that had killed my father had changed me.

I refused to recall those couple of years when I had been real young, when my father had still been alive, and Cade had always been with Aiden and I. Those years when Cade had been my friend and near constant companion, when I had loved him without knowing what love was. It had been such a sweet, simple love between us, freely given and returned.

Then Cade's parents had been killed and he had drifted away into a world of solitude. He had retreated from me completely without ever explaining why. I'd been upset by his actions, but as time moved on I had forgotten about our bond. Until The Freezing had occurred, and we'd been thrust back together, and that love had rushed back.

"Oh, I will."

I had forgotten all about Bishop until he spoke again. I managed a wan smile as I focused my attention back on the doctor. I wanted to believe with him, wanted to believe *in* him, but I didn't really believe in anything anymore. "I hope so doc."

His eyes fixed on me. "Are you ok Bethany?"

"I'm fine," I assured him halfheartedly. My gaze turned toward the dead alien on the counter. "Do you know how it made itself look like that little girl yet?"

Bishop's attention shifted from me to his new favorite toy. "No, not yet, but there are plenty of examples of mimicry in the world. The king snake looks like the coral snake; therefore predators will avoid the king snake for fear that it is poisonous. That's what is known as batesian mimicry. These creatures appear to be displaying both batesian and aggressive mimicry though."

Bishop had moved closer to the creature. For the first time, beneath the awe and incredulity, I saw true unease on his features. I swallowed heavily, discomfited by the look in his eyes. "What's aggressive mimicry?" I inquired.

"It is a form of mimicry where predators share similar traits with something harmless in order to lure in their prey. The alligator snapping turtle uses its pink tongue to lure in fish that believe the tongue is a worm. The fish that try to eat the worm are eaten instead." Much like when Sarah had been lured in to try and help the girl. Goose pimples were beginning to break out on my flesh; I couldn't tear my gaze away from the hideous thing on the counter. "But animals that exhibit aggressive mimicry don't strongly resemble the creature they are trying to lure in, not like the coral and king snake. Not like this thing resembling us.

"This truly is a unique ability; it's unlike anything I've ever seen before. What I don't know is if they were always able to do this, or if this ability is a new development. Have they started to evolve in order to find new ways to capture and kill us?"

My goose bumps were now full on shivers; I could barely breathe through the constriction in my chest. "Is it possible to do that so quickly?" I managed to croak out.

Bishop's eyes were astute. "Not for us, not for any creature we've ever known before…"

"But we don't know these creatures."

"No, we don't. It's ingenious if you think about it, mimicking one of us, especially a child."

I hated the admiration in his tone, not when all I felt was stark terror. "And if they evolved to do this…"

"Then what else can they evolve to do."

I ran to the sink, grasped hold of the edge of it, and dry heaved until my ribs ached. I was sweating profusely as I rinsed my mouth with water and straightened away from the sink. Ashamed of my weakness, I couldn't meet Bishop's gaze as I walked toward the window. It was covered with chicken wire, the reason why I couldn't begin to fathom, but it caused the sunlight streaming through it to dance across the tile floor in a honeycomb pattern.

I didn't know what to say, there were no words for what he had just told me. "It may not be evolution. This may have been a trait of theirs the entire time."

We both knew he was lying, if they had been able to do this from the beginning, they would have. "Who are you trying to kid here Bishop, me or you?"

He pondered this for a minute before answering, "You."

Well at least he was honest, I thought grudgingly. "Do you think the larger ones can do the same, or is it only the smaller ones?"

"I don't know."

There wasn't even a ripple upon the water of the bay as the cloudless sky seemed to blend seamlessly into the ocean's surface. It was difficult to believe that there were so many unknown horrors lurking out there on this tranquil day. "Does it have any weaknesses?"

"Well, you guys managed to kill it, so obviously it has at least one."

I strained not to let my dread show as I turned toward him. "That took a whole lot of bullets Bishop. If it had been closer..." I let the words trail off; we'd both seen what that closeness had done to Sarah. "How are we ever going to defeat them?" I breathed.

"You."

I started in surprise. "What?"

"Your blood Bethany, it *has* to be the answer. There has to be some key within it that will help us to awaken the remaining survivors of The Freezing. The sooner I find it, the more people we can save."

"And the more people we have to help us fight," I whispered. "Strength in numbers."

"But the longer it takes me to find the answer…"

"The more people the aliens will capture, drain, and destroy."

"Yes. We could lose them all before I uncover the truth."

I nodded as his words danced around inside my mind. I may not believe that Bishop was right about me, but he was a lot smarter than I was, and he seemed to be the only hope that mankind had at this point. The only hope for saving so many people and he needed my help to do it. "Ok then, let's get you that equipment doc."

***

"You can't do this Bethany."

I glanced back at Abby as I lifted the rifle onto my back. Darnell handed me a backpack filled with whatever ammo they could spare, and two extra sig sauer pistols. Bret hefted the bag of food onto his back and slipped a revolver and pistol into his waistband. I had tried to talk him out of coming with me, but it had been useless. Private Lloyd Price was also coming with us as was Jenna.

I had tried to talk her out of joining us but once she heard that we were going to attempt to reach the hospital in Plymouth, she had been adamant that she come with us. There was a hospital in Wareham, which was closer, but only by a little bit and in the opposite direction of where Darnell planned to go. I hadn't realized he had an actual destination in mind until he'd informed me of that earlier today, but then there was little I paid attention to anymore. Apparently we were Boston bound in the hopes of encountering more survivors, which he was certain the city would have, along with more weapons.

I didn't know why Jenna was so insistent that she join us, but she wouldn't be dissuaded. I was actually a little grateful to have another person come along. Jenna had also received training with a weapon and in fighting. She may not be as proficient as the rest of us, but she was good enough, and another person who could shoot would come in handy.

"Only use the radio once a day. The rest of us are staying here one more day, and then we'll be heading toward Plymouth also. I don't know how quickly we'll be able to move, but I plan to proceed at a pretty rapid pace. Radio me at eighteen hundred hours every day," Darnell said as he handed the radio and a map to Lloyd.

Lloyd nodded as he clipped the radio to his belt. "Yes sir."

"There's enough food to last a couple of days. I would love to spare more, but..." Molly trailed off, her cute face pinched as she watched us nervously.

Molly had been a stranger to us before this had all happened, but her training in scuba diving had saved our lives when we were trapped on the Cape and unable to escape by crossing either of the bridges. She was a sweet person with her curly auburn hair and green cat eyes. Since we had joined the larger group of survivors, she had begun to aid in the cooking duty, and had taken charge of the food supplies.

What Molly wouldn't say was that they couldn't spare anymore food on us, especially when they didn't know what our fate would be. "We'll be fine," I assured her. "There will be plenty of opportunities to find more food on the way."

Molly managed a feeble smile for me before squeezing my arm. "I'm sure there will be," she replied fervently.

"We'll be following a different route than you, sticking more toward the back roads and heavily wooded areas," Darnell continued.

"We'll meet up with you once we get the supplies we're looking for," Lloyd assured him.

"Bethany please," Abby whispered.

I wrapped my arm around her and pulled her against my side. "I *have* to go Abby, but Aiden will be here."

"You *don't* have to go!" she insisted. "There are others that could go!"

I glanced at my brother over her head. He had wanted to come too, but we couldn't leave Abby alone, and he was more essential here than I was. He understood science, he was a better help to the doc, and was rapidly learning the medical care instruction that Bishop could teach him. Bishop had taken, and stored, plenty of blood from me over the past three weeks. In the past day he had taken even more. He had protested my leaving also, but he'd done so only to me. I think Bishop realized that I had to do this, that I needed some sort of mission and goal if I was going to keep surviving.

I had to have something to help me escape the constant torment I dealt with over losing Cade. "There aren't any others," I said.

"Of course there are!"

"Abigail," I said calmly, but firmly.

"It will be fine," Molly assured her. "I could use some help with the cooking and getting the rest of the supplies packed up."

Abby gave a small nod but tears shimmered in her doe brown eyes. I managed a smile for her and gave her a quick hug. I felt guilty leaving her here, felt guilty upsetting her like this, but it *had* to be done. If we succeeded than we may very well be able to save her life, and the lives of so many others. I didn't like the idea of hurting her, it was the last thing I wanted as she had already experienced so much loss in her short life, but I couldn't stay here.

"I love you Abby."

She threw her arms around me and hugged me. "I love you too Bethany, please come back."

I closed my eyes, fighting against a wave of tears as I dislodged myself from her. I had to get away from her, before I couldn't. "Good luck," Darnell said.

Aiden walked beside me as we exited the building. He took hold of my arm pulling me back from the others as they made their way to the forest. "You know that I don't agree with this."

"Aiden..."

"Even Bishop feels it would be better if you stayed. If something happens to you..."

"He has plenty of my blood, believe me, I know."

"That's not the point..."

"I *have* to do this Aiden."

He was only eighteen, yet dark circles had formed under his eyes. His mouth was pinched; the corners of it were tugged down. Just weeks ago, even with the aliens constantly looming over us in the sky, he had retained a carefree air and youthful innocence that I hadn't possessed in years. Aiden's exuberance had been contagious, his smile lively, and his quick wit uplifting. Though he still retained a lot of his old personality there were subtle changes taking him over that I didn't like. I wanted to ease the burden he had taken on, and this was one of the ways I could do that.

"If you're doing this because of him Bethany..."

"What are you talking about?" I interrupted crossly.

He frowned as he tilted his head; his golden hair was longer than usual as it spilled into one of his eyes. I was struck by how much of a man he'd become in such a short time, by how much he looked like our father. A lump formed in my throat, my eyes burned. I wished our parents could have been here to see the strong, brave, intelligent man he had become. They would have been so proud of him, and Abby. I shied away from thoughts of what they would think about me.

"Anyone with eyes can see the difference in you Bethany. Ever since he was taken, you've been walking around like a zombie." I couldn't meet his gaze; I became focused upon the people gathered by the tree line, waiting for me. "I hope you're not doing this as some sort of a death wish."

I swallowed heavily, my hands fisted at my sides. "I'm doing this because it may be the only hope we have," I gritted through clenched teeth. I was resentful of his words, no matter how truthful they may be. "The doc needs those supplies as soon as possible if he's going to help anyone. This is the best way to get them."

His hand was feathery on my arm; I finally turned my attention back to him. "I understand that, but I also feel as if you don't plan on returning."

My mouth dropped open. "Of course I do!" I sputtered in indignation. "You and Abby…"

"I want you to return for *you*."

I felt as if I'd been slapped as I recoiled from him. "Aiden…"

"I would like *you* to live again. Not for me or Abby, for *you*," he insisted. "He's dead Bethany…"

"Shut up Aiden."

"No, you have to realize that he *is* dead."

I glared at him; my teeth throbbed from clenching them so forcefully. "I *know* that Aiden!" I snarled. Aiden's eyes widened at my shouted confession, he hadn't expected me to tell him that I had come to accept the fact that Cade was gone. "I know he's dead, I know that he's not coming back. I know that I'm alone…" I broke off shaking my head. "Not alone, I didn't mean that. I don't know what I am anymore."

"You're not alone Bethany." To my absolute dismay and shame my chin began to tremble. I was trying not to unravel, not to let my misery show. He was concerned enough about me, I couldn't turn into a sobbing mess right in front of him.

"But I am." I took a deep breath. Regaining control of myself I lifted my chin and met his troubled gaze. "I love you and Abby. I love Bret and Molly, and I've even come to like Jenna a little, but it's not the same. Nothing will *ever* be the same. *I* will never be the same. What I felt for him…"

My gaze drifted back toward the group waiting far more patiently than I would have been. I'd never talked about my feelings for Cade, never shared them with anyone. I didn't think they could understand the intense bond that had been forged between us in such a short time. Especially since I had been dating Bret when everything with Cade happened. I felt they would think I was being childish, or that I felt guilty because Cade had sacrificed himself to save me (which I did), but it was so much more than all of those things. My love for Cade was the first really amazing thing I had experienced in years. It had been so different, so *true* that I could feel the strength of it all the way to the center of my soul.

"I loved him Aiden. I loved him with every ounce of my being. I loved him with a joy and intensity that I never even knew could exist." I turned my gaze back to my brother. He had to understand that I wasn't a silly child harboring an intense crush, or a damaged person with survivor's guilt. "I knew what soul mate meant with Cade."

Though I knew Aiden loved me, and realized that I was far more mature than almost anybody my age, I could see the pity in his gaze. It was that exact look that was the reason I had never talked about my feelings for Cade. "I know that the two of you went through some intense shared experiences…"

"Don't." I interrupted briskly. "Don't you *dare* minimize what happened between us. I am *telling* you what I feel for him, what I will *always* feel for him. I am telling you what was, is, and always will be. I loved him from the first time I saw him, I loved him when he first taught me to fish, and when he insisted that I be allowed to play with the two of you. I loved him when he was broken by his parent's deaths and started avoiding us. The night of our father's funeral he came and sat with me in the garden for hours. It was the first time I'd spoken with him in two years."

"I didn't know that," Aiden whispered.

"Throughout that whole horrendous time he was the first and only person I cried in front of."

Aiden's gaze took on that analytical skepticism I'd seen when he examined bones or dissected animals. "I didn't know you had cried."

"He didn't come back after that night. At first I kept going to the garden, hoping that he would return, but he never did. I was wounded by his rejection in the beginning but time, and the struggle that our lives became, eased it. Eventually I forgot about that night, eventually I moved on. Eventually I even started dating Bret, but you know how much I resisted that, how platonic our relationship truly was. At first I didn't understand why it was like that, why *I* was like that. Every girl in school thought I was crazy for not agreeing to go out with Bret right away, and then for being so distant with him once I did."

"Bethany…"

"And then Cade *touched* me Aiden." I couldn't stop now, once I'd opened the bottle on the emotions I'd been suppressing, I couldn't stop them from pouring out of me. I grabbed hold of his hand, desperate for him to understand, desperate for him to see *why* I was so broken. And maybe, just maybe, he could even forgive me for being so lost. He had to know that I hadn't abandoned him or Abby, that I didn't *want* to die. He had to know that I simply couldn't breathe, or even *be* anymore, because a part of me had been lost forever with Cade.

"Then Cade pulled me into that antique store, and held me, and he kissed me…" I broke off uncertain of how to proceed. "And *everything* made sense. I was whole for the first time in awhile, whole in a way I never knew I could be. My indistinct feelings toward Bret, the strange emptiness inside of me, it all made sense because what I had been missing this entire time was Cade. With him it was so easy, so beautiful, and so *absolute.* Even my guilt, and the lingering sorrow over surviving that car wreck when dad didn't, weren't anywhere near as bad when he was holding me. With him everything was better, even with the world falling apart around us.

"My love for him is *true* Aiden, you must believe that. You also have to believe that though I'm empty without him, I will do everything I can to come back to you and Abby. I love you; I don't want either of you to experience anymore pain. I'm broken, but I *will* survive and I will continue to keep on living. Please believe me when I tell you that I do *not* have a death wish."

Aiden's eyes were filled with tears, tears I knew he would later shed for Cade and I. Tears that I was still unable to shed for us. "I didn't know Bethany."

"I know."

"I'm sorry. I would love to take this from you, I really would. I'm your older brother, I should be protecting you. I should be the stronger one of the two of us, not you."

I frowned at him, confused by his words. "But you *are* the stronger one Aiden."

"You saw dad die, and you never cried. You saw Cade die, and you never cried." I winced at his words, shying away from the awful memories they aroused. "You *are* the stronger one Bethany."

I bit on my bottom lip as I shook my head. "No Aiden. That just makes me the colder one."

The sadness in his eyes was almost more than I could tolerate. I embraced him tightly, knowing that I had to leave before I couldn't. "I love you Bethy," he said as he cradled my head.

"I love you too Aiden. I'll see you soon."

"I know."

CHAPTER 4

    With just the four of us, we made pretty good time. If the terrain allowed, there were times we were able to jog for a couple of miles before having to take a break. Lloyd would have been able to make even better time without us, but he never became irritated with our slower abilities. It would be great if we could do it all in one day, but I knew eventually we would become tired, hungry, and more than likely come across some threat.
    I still held out some small hope that we wouldn't run into anything. The sooner this was over and done with, the happier I would be. Jenna was the first to tire. She had changed a lot from when the aliens had first attacked, but she had always been a girly girl and some habits were tough to break. Physical exercise still wasn't one of her favorite things, but she'd been trying to adapt to our new world. That was the only reason I didn't become annoyed when she asked if we could take a break after only eight miles.
    She was panting as she settled onto the ground and used the back of her arm to wipe the sweat from her brow. I still didn't understand why she'd insisted on coming with us in the first place, but I wasn't going to push her. There were things I preferred to keep secret also. Maybe she had simply sought to escape the warehouse, and the people, for a bit. I had a feeling it had more to do with wanting to stay near Bret, but she hadn't pursued the renewal of that relationship after our break up. Though I suspected she stayed away because Bret was mistakenly convinced that we would get back together again one day.
    Bret handed Jenna and I each a bottle of water and a power bar. The sun was at its zenith in the sky. Its rays filtered through the trees in flickering bits that reminded me of how I had imagined fairies dancing amongst the beams

as a child. I felt a real smile as I bit into my power bar and tilted my head back to let the sun warm my face.

"I think we should rest for a couple of hours now. We'll move again later on in the day," Lloyd said.

"We can't move as fast at night."

"We can't move as fast in the heat either," Lloyd retorted.

I frowned but nodded my agreement. He was right, it was September but the day was unseasonably warm. The heat would drain our energy, and cause us to dehydrate, far faster than any of us wanted. I settled down against a tree and closed my eyes. I hadn't slept much last night, but I knew I wouldn't sleep at all now. Sleep was a lost commodity to me, one that I'd given up on awhile ago. I'd actually gotten quite good at dealing with the depravation, though I would have welcomed at least a couple of minutes of rest. Anymore time than that and the dreams would start. Dreams that, while comforting at the time, left me lost and broken and aching for something I couldn't ever have again when I awoke.

I listened to the sounds of the birds and squirrels moving through the trees, reassured and lulled by their presence. I had learned in the beginning that when the aliens were near, the animals became eerily silent. Apparently *they* were even terrified of the monsters lurking about.

It was all so peaceful right now, it was nearly perfect. If only…

And then Cade was sitting beside me, his midnight hair fell over his defined, handsome features. His onyx eyes gleamed in the filtering light of the day. There was sadness in his gaze, but also a love so deep that I felt it to the very core of my being. "Bethany," he breathed. His strong, calloused hands ran deliciously over my skin as he shifted closer. I could feel the heat of his lean, muscled body against mine. Shivers of delight raced over me, I could hardly breathe past the need pulsing through my veins. "*My* Bethany."

Tears choked me. "Yes," I agreed, unable to do anything else because it was so unbelievably true. I *was* his, I would *always* be his. "I'm dreaming again aren't I?"

It had been awhile since he had haunted my dreams, awhile since I had even slept long enough to have a dream. I must have fallen asleep for far longer than I'd anticipated. It was odd how aware I was of these facts right now. This was a dream, he wasn't real, it would all go away, but it was all so delightfully perfect right now that I didn't care.

"You are," he confirmed.

"I miss you, so much." My voice cracked on the words, his thumb wiped away the tear that slid free. "I'm broken without you."

"You're not broken Bethany, you're just bruised. You've been here before, you will survive this too."

"I know. I know I will. I just wish you were here. All the *time* I wish you were here."

His lips were tender against my cheeks as he kissed my tears away. His hands slid through my hair as he pulled me closer. Those lips, those wondrously marvelous and warm lips were everything that I remembered as my heart hammered in eager anticipation. I felt the brush of them in every fiber of my being as warmth spread out from the point of contact. The heat seeped through my body, warming all of my frozen cells. The delicious scent of earth and something almost primal engulfed me as I inhaled the aroma of him.

"I wish I was here too."

A small sob escaped me, and then his lips were desperate and eager upon mine, and nothing else mattered. My heart leapt and soared in my chest, everything within me screamed for so much more. I melted against him with every intention of never releasing his solid arms again as my mind spun with happiness and yearning. Even though I knew this wasn't real, that it couldn't last, I allowed myself to be swept up in the ecstasy that filled me.

I found I could actually breathe again as his tongue swept in to take possession of my mouth. His hands found my cheeks, my neck, and my collarbone before stroking over my arms once more. He moved suddenly, lifting me and settling me into his lap. His hand entangled in my hair as he pulled my head back, his lips traveling over my throat sent shivers coursing through my body.

"*My* Bethany," he whispered again.

I was crying freely now, I couldn't stop it as pleasure and regret encompassed me. "Yes," I agreed over and over. "Forever," I vowed.

He reluctantly pulled away from me. I hated the heartache and loss in his eyes. "You must hold onto your hope Bethany."

"I can't hope for you to return anymore, it's too much." I could barely speak through the agony wrenching at my soul. "I'll always love you, but I have to let myself grieve for you now. I must."

His fingers stroked over my cheeks, his head tilted to the side. He was magnificent, heartbreakingly handsome, and he was *mine*. Even if he was gone forever, he would always be mine. "I didn't say hope for me Bethany. You must grieve me, you must let me go one day, but you have to hold onto *your* hope."

"I have no hope anymore," I breathed.

"Of course you do. You wouldn't be here, and you wouldn't be doing *this*, if you didn't. You must hold onto it and use it to get you through these difficult times."

I frowned at him, not understanding what he meant, and then I got it. "I *do* have hope for mankind. I *do* have hope that we will survive."

He robbed my breath when he flashed his heartbreaking smile and rested his forehead briefly against mine. "I know you do, and as long as you hold onto that hope you will survive."

I frowned; his words had broken the small bubble of bliss I'd discovered in this dream world. "Of course you know," I whispered through the growing lump in my throat. "This is only a dream, you're only my subconscious. Of course you know that there is hope still within me, even if I hadn't realized it until now."

Sadness crept over him, his hands slid through my honey colored hair as he spread it before us. In the real world my hair wasn't loose; it was tied back in a long braid and twisted into a bun in order to keep it from tangling too badly. It also wasn't this clean as regular showers and baths were a luxury that we didn't have any more. I was glad that it was gleaming and shiny in this world though. I didn't care if he was real or not, I was determined to look as good as I possibly could for him, no matter what.

"Beautiful," he whispered. "My beautiful Bethany."

I closed my eyes. Even if I didn't agree with his words, especially next to his masculine perfection, they were wonderful to hear. My nose was a little too pointy, my face still round, full, and babyish even though I'd lost weight. I was too skinny, awkward, and clumsy. There was no grace, no perfection about me, but in Cade's eyes there was. Or at least there *had* been. I knew that with absolute certainty. Even with all of my imperfections he had found me beautiful, and he had loved me.

I opened my eyes, blinking away my tears as I tried to focus on his beloved face. "My magnificent Cade."

That striking grin was back. It was even more beautiful for the rarity with which it had existed in real life. "If you say so."

"I know so."

His hand stilled in my hair, he bent to kiss me again. "It's almost time for me to go, but you must remember what I said. You can do this Bethany; you can succeed where others wouldn't. You're so much stronger than you even realize. I know your soul, your heart, and though you're suffering now, you'll one day bring the pieces back together."

"The biggest piece will always be missing." His eyes searched my face as his fingers caressed my cheeks. Though this was my dream, his anguish and longing seemed almost real, almost *palpable*. Once again I was struck by the strange reality of this dream. His need for me and for everything we'd had and everything we'd lost was there. I could feel it. His torment beat against me so fiercely that I felt I had to say something to try and ease it. "But I can put the rest of the puzzle together," I tried to assure him.

"I love you Bethany."

I buried myself against him, clinging to him as I pressed my face into his neck and cried freely. I had never said those words to him in life, it was something that I would always regret, but I said them now, and I said them repeatedly, and enthusiastically. I hoped that somehow he would be able to hear them, that somewhere a piece of him still existed and could feel the genuine outpouring of my love for him.

He rocked me soothingly as he kissed my neck and cheeks. "I must go."

"Not yet," I breathed. "Please just one minute more."

But it was too late; I could already feel him drifting toward a place where I would never see him again. I was acutely aware of the fact that he wouldn't be returning. Another sob wrenched from me, I fought to retain my hold on him, but he was already beyond my reach. Forever.

***

"Bethany, come on Bethany, wake up."

I struggled to break free of the sleep clinging to me. I didn't want to wake up, I knew what awaited me there, but it was impossible to fight the inevitable. I opened my eyes to find Jenna kneeling before me; her bright green eyes shimmered with worry. I turned away from the sorrowful look in her eyes, unable to stand the pity there as I angrily wiped the tears from my face. I was ashamed that she had seen me cry, ashamed that she had seen me so vulnerable and weak.

"Are you ok?" she asked softly.

I quickly glanced around but I didn't see Bret or Lloyd. "Where are they?"

Jenna glanced over her shoulder. "They went to scout ahead." That was a relief; at least they hadn't seen me crying like a baby over a dream. "Bret wanted to give you a chance to sleep a little more. Bethany…"

"I'm fine." I realized that was the first time I had said it and felt as if it might actually be true, or at least not a completely bold faced lie. Cade had been killed, I still lived, and there still was, and always would be, hope. I sat up straighter against the tree.

Jenna rested her hand on my shoulder to stop me before I could rise. I frowned at her, unable to understand the sympathy in her eyes. Jenna and I had run in completely different circles in school, and her disdain of everything that I was had always been obvious. As had her desire for Bret. We'd started to get along a little better over the past few weeks, I would grieve for her if something were to happen to her, but I wouldn't exactly consider her a friend.

"Why are you being so nice to me?" I inquired.

Jenna sighed as she sat beside me. She dropped her chin to her knees for a brief moment before turning to me. "I was mean to you in high school," she admitted. "I know that, but it was all so petty, and silly, and... high school." She snorted as she shook her head and dropped her arm over her knees. "It seems so long ago, so pointless and stupid."

"It does," I agreed.

"I was so foolish." Her strawberry colored hair drifted forward in the breeze. She tucked it loosely behind her ear. She was far more petite than I, with a full mouth and a nose most plastic surgeons would envy. She'd been perfect in high school, the golden girl with manicured nails, styled hair, and high priced clothes. It was not the same girl sitting beside me now, though I noticed her nails were still a pretty pink color. I smiled over the simple, small gesture to retain something from her old life. I knew how she felt; I was clinging to as much as I could too, but everyday it seemed as if there was less and less to hold onto. "It was so easy back then though," she breathed.

I thought back to those days, the ones where my mom was still alive, and I was dating Bret. The aliens had hovered over our city my entire junior year, but after the first few months a false sense of security had settled over everyone, even while the aliens had been stripping us of our rights, and our freedoms. We had all been so foolish, so silly to even remotely think they meant well, but hindsight was twenty-twenty, and there was no changing the past. We could still change the future though.

"I'm sorry for the way I was back then."

My gaze slid toward her as I tried to keep my disbelief hidden. "It's ok."

"No, I was mean to you and I am sorry for that. It was just that…"

"You like Bret."

Her lips quirked as she smiled wistfully. "Yeah, I do."

"And you were used to getting whatever you wanted."

She chuckled. "I certainly wasn't used to losing a guy to someone like you. No offense."

I grinned at her as I brushed back a lose strand of hair. "None taken, I never understood it either. We're not together anymore, why haven't you gone after him?"

She shrugged indifferently, but sadness crept over her. "Cause he still loves you."

"But..."

"It's ok. I think he'll come around one day, or I'll move on. Maybe we can even find some cute survivors somewhere," she added nonchalantly.

"Jenna..."

"Right now we all need each other. When all of this first happened, I didn't get that. I kept waiting to wake up, kept waiting for the punch line, kept waiting for it all not to be real. But there is no punch line, and all we have is each other. Trying to get Bret to notice me isn't a priority anymore."

I was startled by how much she had grown up in these past few weeks. How much she had changed. But then, she had lost both of her parents in the attack. She didn't say it, but I knew that she held onto some hope they were still alive. Not that I blamed her. She hadn't seen either of them die, didn't even know if they had been frozen, and if Bishop's blood type theory was correct then at least one of her parents, perhaps both, had escaped The Freezing. There was still a chance they might be alive.

"If there is one thing I've learned, it's that we don't know how much time we have left. It could end today for all we know. Getting Bret to notice you may not be a priority, but I would at least tell him how you feel. I love Bret, he's a great friend, but he can be a bit obtuse about some things," I told her.

"You mean like his firm belief that you will eventually get over Cade."

I tried to cover my involuntary flinch over Cade's name, but I knew she had seen it. "Yes, like that."

Jenna heaved a breath, forced a small smile, and climbed to her feet. "You're right about not knowing how much time is left, but Bret needs some time to come to terms with losing you. I also need time. We've lost a lot, this isn't our world anymore."

"No, it's not." I took hold of the hand she offered me and squeezed it. I'd lost all my friends, but I felt like I might have found a friend where I'd never thought I would. "I'm glad we had this talk."

She grinned at me. "Me too."

CHAPTER 5

It was tougher to move through the night, especially without a flashlight, but I felt strangely safer with only the moon and stars to guide us. It was stupid to feel that way, we'd been attacked more than once at night, but I couldn't help it. Though it was harder to see, we made good time and reached the edge of Plymouth before daybreak.

Lloyd consulted the map. "We can cut through Myles Standish; use the state forest as cover. It's only seven miles but the terrain will slow us down."

"And we'd..." Jenna's eyes were distant as she broke off.

I frowned at her, but it was Bret that asked the question. "And we'd what?"

Jenna bit on her bottom lip as her shoulders slumped. "I might as well tell you," she mumbled. I bristled, disliking the fact she had kept anything from us, especially after our talk earlier. "I wrote a note for my parents before I left. I told them that I would try to meet them in Plymouth at my Aunt Lucy's house. If they're still alive..."

Her voice trailed off, the underlying hope within it was nearly tangible. "They would go to your Aunt Lucy's," I finished for her.

"Yes," she breathed, tears shimmered in her vivid eyes.

"Where does she live?"

"State road, it's only four miles from the hospital, but..."

"But it's four miles out of the way," Lloyd finished for her.

His annoyance and impatience were evident as he blatantly glared at Jenna. She shifted nervously, looking guilty and frightened, but she showed no signs of backing down. I didn't blame her. If I thought there was a chance my mother was still alive, I would do anything I could to get to her.

I could cut the tension in the air with a knife as we stared at each other. "Well it won't hurt us to try and get there," I said.

"That is *not* the mission!" Lloyd barked.

"Lloyd…"

"We were given explicit instructions on our goal, and our approach."

I was startled by Lloyd's insistence, but then again I had never been through boot camp, or military training. As far as he was concerned he had his orders and he was going to obey them. Jenna looked stricken as her eyes flitted over all of us. "We were never told which route to take," I said in an attempt to make him see reason.

"We were told to take the safest and most direct route possible. This isn't even on course."

My patience was quickly unraveling. Jenna had a chance to see if her family was still alive, and we were going to take it. "Her parent's lives…"

"Our lives, the lives of *many*!" Lloyd interrupted angrily. "The needs of many greatly outweigh the needs of a few."

"Lloyd!"

His air of youthfulness vanished as he leveled me with a withering glare that caused me to take an involuntary step back. "I am not the bad guy here. *You* are the one that was determined to do this mission, and we *will* do it."

"It's only a small detour."

"It's a detour through more populated roads."

I looked helplessly at Bret and Jenna. Bret was thoughtful, his hands clasped behind his back as he rocked on his heels. Jenna looked about ready to cry, but there was a growing air of indignation around her. "I'll go by myself."

"No one is going anywhere by themselves!" I told her. "Lloyd…"

"This is not a democracy."

"We are *not* in the military!" I snapped at him.

Lloyd's jaw locked. "I am, and I have my orders."

"Enough!" Bret finally inserted. "We are not separating; we are not deviating from the mission. Part of our goal was to try and find survivors. Jenna has a lead on where we could find some people who aren't frozen. It *is* part of the mission Lloyd, it may take us a little longer, but it is still part of the mission."

I couldn't stop the admiration and relief that filled me as I turned to Bret. I would have sat here and butted heads with Lloyd for hours until one of us just gave up or I completely lost my temper. Leave it to Bret to find reason and logic to use against the stubborn soldier.

"We cannot leave here knowing that we chance leaving survivors behind," Bret continued, his tone level and encouraging.

Lloyd thought over Bret's reasoning before nodding. "You're right," he finally relented. "We can't leave the area without first seeking out the possible survivors."

I breathed a sigh of relief, Jenna let out a small cry of delight and she impulsively threw her arms around Bret. I bit back a smile at Bret's look of disbelief as he awkwardly managed to hug her back. "Address?" Lloyd barked out.

Jenna was beet red and grinning beautifully as she pulled away from Bret and rattled off the address.

***

I was regretting our decision and the fact that we were now standing on the edge of the main street in Plymouth. There were trees lining the road but they weren't much coverage, and the two and three story buildings offered no protection from anything above. A few of the buildings were nothing more than piles of brick and wood. I didn't have to ponder what had been capable of doing that, I'd been unfortunate enough to watch one of the larger octopus/tick/jellyfish things level the antique store our mother had been in the basement of.

Lloyd was studying the map for an alternate route, but everything seemed to be miles out of the way and we had already lost a day just getting this far. "Maybe if we wait till night," Jenna suggested.

"There will still be no cover," Lloyd retorted.

The hair on my arms stood on end as I took in the awnings, debris, and open doorways. I had made it down a street even more open than this once, and nearly been caught. Cade had saved me...

My hands fisted as I forcefully shut the thought down. There was no Cade anymore; I would have to save myself this time, and every time after this. We had to save each other. No matter what, I wasn't going to give up the hope of possibly finding Jenna's parents. "We can do it," I insisted. "Under cover of night, and using the buildings, we can do this."

"Bethany..." Bret started.

"Look," I pointed to the street, to the piles of rubble, to the vast amount of stores and restaurants with their doors thrust open. "In the sun there doesn't appear to be a lot of hiding places, but under darkness and hiding behind the debris, we can move through the town."

"Bethany," Bret said again.

Even Jenna looked unconvinced as she studied the street like it might bite her. "We can go back, go to the hospital first, and then try my aunt's," she suggested.

"That will easily take another day or more," Lloyd muttered.

I glanced toward the sky, but the large ship that had settled over Boston over a year ago wasn't visible from here, and the smaller ones didn't seem to be about. It was tough to tell with them though; they were soundless, and as fast as any racecar. I searched the woods, but birds still chirruped within the trees and there was a chipmunk searching for an acorn at the nearby base of a tree. There didn't appear to be any imminent threat, but my skin began to crawl.

"We either double back or go through," Lloyd said.

"The animals are still out, I think we're relatively safe until nightfall," I pointed out.

"And then all bets are off," Lloyd said.

The day stretched endlessly onward, the movement of the sun seemed excruciatingly sluggish as it shifted position in the sky. I tried to rest but my mind wouldn't shut off. I kept opening my eyes to stare down the street. I had sounded confident when I'd said we could make it down there but I wasn't so sure anymore. The more I studied it, the less hiding places there seemed to be.

Unable to take sitting still anymore I stood up and stretched my back. Bret's eyes followed me as I anxiously paced toward a scraggly looking pine and leaned against it. I didn't want to look at the street anymore, but my eyes were inexorably drawn to it. I felt as if there was something I wasn't seeing.

I may have grown up nearby, but I didn't know Plymouth all that well. For one thing it was huge, and for another I'd avoided riding in cars after surviving the accident that had killed my father. I hadn't gone on the school fieldtrips to Plimoth Plantation, or the Mayflower II, so I probably knew even less about the town than most of the kids I'd gone to school with.

"Has the town always looked like this?" I asked Bret. "Minus the damage of course."

Bret studied the street before shrugging absently. "More or less, I mean there were always people and tourists moving about, but I'm sure it hasn't been busy like that for awhile."

It began to dawn on me what exactly was wrong with this town. "There's nothing left," I breathed.

Bret's forehead was furrowed as he rose to his feet. I'd thought that Jenna was sleeping, but one of her eyes popped open. Lloyd had been standing guard fifty feet away, but he came closer as he heard our words. "What do you mean?" Bret inquired.

Horror flowed through me as I stared at the empty street. "There's nothing there. Every other street we've come across, in *every* other town, has had something left behind. Bicycles, shoes, hell we'd even come across shirts and pants, socks and underwear. There have been wallets, money, and change. There have been toupees and wigs; there have even been dentures, but there is nothing out *there*. There isn't one thing on those streets except for debris from the buildings."

Lloyd let out a harsh breath. "You're right."

"But what does that mean?" Jenna asked tremulously.

I shook my head; I had no answer for that question.

"They're cleaning it up." We all turned toward Lloyd who had the look of someone that had just seen a bunch of pixies dancing down the street.

"Excuse me?" I asked.

"They've cleaned the town up; rid it of the debris left behind by us. Cleaning it so that they can…"

"So they can what?" Bret's question hung heavy in the air as Lloyd's voice trailed off.

"So they can move in," I suggested. I had only meant it to be a lame joke, but I suddenly felt trapped beneath the weight of their horrified gazes. "Oh crap, you don't think that's it, do you?"

"What else could it be?" Jenna questioned. "Why else would they bother to come back and sweep the streets clean of all possessions? They don't need the money, I doubt they want the wigs, and I'm certain they aren't looking for dentures. We had all assumed that they would just leave after they collected and killed as many of us as possible. What if they plan to stay after?"

I recoiled from the thought as I grappled not to give into the panic beginning to thrum through my veins. I hadn't even considered the possibility that they might stay behind after they were done destroying us. They had rarely come to earth, even when they had been pretending peace, the last thing I had expected was for them to stay. They had seemed to openly disdain our planet, and it was more than obvious they only sought us for our blood. Maybe they hadn't come down often because of the fact that Earth had possessed us repellent human beings.

Bret cursed loudly as he paced away. He ran a hand anxiously through his disordered hair as he cursed violently again. "I always thought they hated it here," Jenna said.

"There is another possibility," Lloyd hedged. Our attention focused on him as we waited breathlessly for any explanation other than the one I had offered. "It is possible that they cleaned the streets because they are using Plymouth as some sort of base for the area. It's a large town, and it's on one of the main routes to Boston from the Cape and surrounding areas. If people are looking to flee the Cape, and surrounding towns, many of them will come through here."

It took everything I had to keep standing; I did require a pine tree to lean against though as I felt my legs begin to shake.

"They wouldn't like to have any human things littering the street, reminding them of our pathetic existence." I was getting to the point where I would really prefer Lloyd to just stop speaking. If he was right then we had just walked right out of the frying pan and into the fire. If he was right, then not only was our mission going to fail, but there was a good chance we might not escape from here. "This could be the lion's den."

Yep, I wanted him to stop speaking. I sensed he might be right though, that they *did* intend to use Plymouth as a base, or perhaps some kind of storage area. It seemed far more feasible than the idea that the aliens might actually *choose* to take up residence on our planet when all of this was over.

"I'm sorry," Jenna whispered.

I swallowed heavily. "It's not your fault," I told her. "There was no way any of us could have known."

I waited for Lloyd to say I told you so, but to his credit, he didn't. He strode away from us to consult the map again.

"I don't think they're around now," I said. "They might plan to move in, but I don't think they're here now."

"Why?" Jenna inquired.

I pointed to the seagulls and heron sitting upon the railings of a boat dock. A few gulls were circling high up in the sky, and a stray dog had appeared at the end of the road. The dog sniffed at one of the piles of rubble in search of some food for its emaciated frame. Within the trees the squirrels, chipmunks, sparrows, blue jays, and robins continued to move about. "The animals always become still when they're near. They're just as afraid of the aliens, and their creatures, as we are."

Lloyd stopped pacing to rejoin us. "We have to go now," he said briskly.

"What?" Jenna demanded. "Are you crazy!?"

"Bethany's right." He pulled the rifle from his back and clasped it firmly. "They aren't here right now, the animals would know. We might not be able to say the same thing in another hour, or even another ten minutes. We have to move now, and we have to move fast."

"Hell," Bret breathed.

"It's still light out," Jenna protested.

"It's our best chance," Lloyd replied hurriedly. "We have to move *now* when we know they're not here."

"Oh crap," I muttered. "Oh crap, oh crap, oh crap."

"Exactly. Stay low and move fast. Keep an eye out for anything unusual, and especially watch the animals. Let's move."

I took a deep breath as I fought against the apprehension trying to take me over. It was now or never, and if we didn't go now, there may very well be a never. I gathered every ounce of courage I had, tightened my grip on my rifle and took a deep breath to steady my nerves.

I fell in behind Lloyd, with Jenna close on my heels and Bret right behind her. We were half bent over as we rushed into the open. A few birds were spooked by our emergence and the sound of their rapid flight caused me to wince involuntarily. I held my breath in preparation for some kind of attack, but as we made it to the shadowed safety of the first building I inhaled a ragged, somewhat relieved breath.

We had made it further than I'd expected in broad daylight, but there were still miles to go. My heart was hammering like a woodpecker on speed and even in the cool September air I was beginning to sweat profusely. I wiped my forehead with the back of my arm as I tried to control my shaking.

We moved swiftly down three empty storefronts before Lloyd disappeared into one of the open doorways. I was breathing heavily as I leaned against the wall inside the building. My eyes scanned over the bar, the stools, and the large glass mirror that accented the bottles lining the shelves. I stared at those bottles, amazed that they were still in one piece upon the shelves and still so perfectly aligned.

The stools had been tossed aside; restaurant tables were upended and splintered into pieces. Streaks of blood marred the wood floors and scratch ticket machine in the corner. The cash register had fallen off the counter, its contents were scattered around the floor before the bar. No one had touched the money and I didn't go for it now. What was the point?

Yet, even with all the destruction and obvious death, those bottles remained completely perfect. It made my skin crawl.

Lloyd broke away, skirting around the chairs and broken tables as he stalked behind the bar. He studied the shelves before pulling a nearly full bottle of whiskey down. "What are you doing?" Bret demanded as Lloyd slipped it into his backpack.

"We make it through this I'm going to have a celebratory drink."

That sounded like a good plan to me and I'd never really liked the taste of alcohol. Lloyd opened the swinging kitchen door with the tip of his rifle and held it ajar as he craned his head to see inside. He nodded to Bret to follow him before disappearing through the doors.

I turned my attention back to the hushed street. The dog had made its way toward us. Now that it was closer I could tell that it appeared to be some kind of lab/shepherd mix. Its coat was matted and its ears hung lopsidedly as it stared at me with soulful eyes. I wanted to call it to us, to pet it and offer it some comfort and love, but I was frightened that its attention to us might be noticed by something else, something far more sinister.

Unfortunately, the dog spotted us. Its head lifted, its limpid brown eyes focused on me as one of its dangly ears rose. My pulse rate increased, I wanted the dog to come to us, and I desperately wanted it to leave all at the same time. *Please*, I silently prayed, though I didn't know if I was praying for it to stay or for it to go.

Drawn by the potential of food, comfort, and companionship the animal began to approach with its head low and its ears drooping. I couldn't think about what the animal had endured that made it so hesitant. I knelt as it crept through the door, my hand stretched out as it moved closer with its tail between its legs. It sniffed at me, but still didn't touch me as it stopped a few feet away.

"Careful Bethany," Jenna urged.

Its wet nose bumped against my hand, it backed away again and then it was pressing closer to me. My hand dug through its tangled fur and brushed over its collar. Its tags clinked as I wrapped my arms around it and hugged it to me. I could feel the pointed edge of its bones through its thick fur as it pressed closer. My heart ached for the poor animal but its coat was one of the most wonderful things I'd felt in awhile. In this small, emaciated creature I felt a kindred wounded and forsaken soul. I pulled away from the dog and tugged its tags toward me.

The dog's ears cocked as I whispered his name, "Barney." Then his tongue licked over my face and he buried himself against me again. For some strange reason tears welled up in my eyes as I buried my face in the dog's neck. Barney had lost people that loved and cared for him also, he had been completely alone, until now.

I pulled back from him as Lloyd and Bret emerged from the kitchen. Lloyd's clear blue eyes narrowed on Barney and I, he frowned as he eyed the dog. Bret offered a half smile, but his eyes looked troubled as he glanced toward the doorway. "We found some stale bread, not the best but better than nothing."

I held out my hand for a piece of bread. Lloyd stared at me before eyeing Barney again. I thought he was going to protest, thought the soldier in him was going to come rearing back to life, but he didn't offer any complaint. He simply broke off a piece of bread and handed it to me. I gave him a small smile as I took the stale bread and held it out to Barney. He sniffed it cautiously before gently taking it from my hand.

"Take his collar off," Lloyd ordered briskly. I nodded as I slipped the jingling collar from Barney's thin neck and dropped it on the counter. "We should get moving if we're going to make it through this town."

CHAPTER 6

We darted in and out of buildings and hid within the shadows as we rapidly moved down the streets. Lloyd and Bret searched another restaurant but came up with only more stale bread and frozen hamburger patties. After that crappy gathering, it was determined to just skip searching the restaurants in an attempt to make it down the street faster.

Lloyd took the lead; he maintained a conversation with gestures alone as we moved steadily forward. Barney stayed close by my side, his ears perked as he listened for danger. It made no sense but I felt oddly safer with him next to me, there wasn't much Barney could do, but I knew he would sense any threat long before we did.

Lloyd stopped as he reached the end of the street. He held his hand to halt us as he poked his head around the corner of the building. He nodded briskly toward us. I took a deep breath before plunging into the open behind Lloyd. It was only thirty feet until we hit the woods again, but it seemed more like thirty miles as we were completely exposed. My heart hammered, my lungs burned as I pushed my legs to their limits of speed and endurance. I'd never run so fast in my life but I didn't think it was going to be fast enough, that I was going to be spotted before I made it to the shelter of the forest.

Lloyd plummeted into the woods and disappeared from sight. I unhesitatingly followed behind him, not caring where he had disappeared to or what might be waiting for me. I only cared that I wasn't on the street anymore. The drop down was further than I had expected. The ground fell out from underneath me, my arms pin-wheeled as I fell a good eight feet through the air. Lloyd was already rolling out of my way and climbing to his feet.

An involuntary grunt escaped me as I landed hard. My ankles throbbed but I was falling, rolling as I tumbled over. Lloyd grabbed hold of me and pulled me out of the way in time for Jenna, and then Bret to land. Barney simply trotted down the side of the embankment, his tongue lolling as his eyes seemed to laugh at us.

"Let's go," Lloyd ordered briskly.

"How much further is it?" Jenna asked.

Lloyd pulled out the map as he began to jog through the woods. "Two point eight miles. We can be there in about half an hour if we hurry."

I was exhausted but the possibility of finally reaching one of our destinations was far too tempting to slow me down. Barney stayed close by my side as he panted. There was a lively step in the dog's gait that hadn't been there when he'd been wandering the street. Apparently a simple piece of bread and a little affection were all he needed to be happy again. I was heartened by his presence and took strength in his determination and joyful attitude.

I turned my attention from Barney to find Lloyd watching me. "Hope he doesn't bark," Lloyd muttered.

I hadn't thought of that, but I wasn't going to respond to Lloyd. Following the map we came across a small back road lined with trees and white picket fences. I was struck with the feeling that we were on the edge of a stage and looking at the scenery from some play. It was so still, so calm and free of debris that it robbed me of my breath.

"Scary," Bret muttered.

I seconded that. Barney sat at my side as I crouched down to rest my fingertips on the ground. The scent of dirt and rotten leaves assaulted me. I inhaled deeply savoring in the raw scent of the earth. *My* earth.

"That's my aunt's house," Jenna breathed pointing at a cheery yellow house with mellow blue shutters. The potted plants hanging from the porch beams swayed in the subtle September breeze playing with the hair on the back of my neck. Their ends were already wilting and brown from lack of water. The whole thing was so peculiar that I was tempted to turn and bolt back into the forest. This air of pristine perfection didn't seem right, not at all.

I glanced at Barney, but he wasn't nervous about the strange road. "The dog seems to think it's ok," Lloyd said.

"Barney."

"What?"

"His name is Barney," I told him.

Lloyd rolled his eyes as he turned his attention back to the road. "*Barney* thinks it's ok."

"Then let's go," Jenna said forcefully.

"Wait." Lloyd held out a hand as he glanced first one way and than the other. "This whole thing…"

"Is just wrong," I finished for him.

His eyes came toward me and he nodded briskly. "It appears safe and we can't stay here," Bret said. "We either move now or we stay here until…"

"Until we know it's not safe," Jenna retorted.

I rested my hand on her arm, looking to calm the simmering tension radiating from her. Her patience was wearing thin and I didn't blame her. "We're going," I assured her. "It may not feel right but it's not going to get any calmer than this road. We have to go."

Lloyd nodded but his eyes were distant and wary. I rose to my full height, if he wasn't going to go first then I would. I took a deep breath and drew on my courage as I prepared to plummet into the calm streets of what had the eerie appearance of Mayberry.

I bolted forward before anyone could stop me, and raced across the street with more speed than I would have possessed a month ago. I felt the thump of the rifle against my back as I took the porch steps two at a time in leaping bounds. I didn't hesitate at the door, didn't even stop to think it might be locked as I grasped hold of the knob and flung it open.

In my hectic pace I nearly fell into the house as I tripped and stumbled over the doorframe. I just barely managed to catch my balance before I slammed into the kitchen table with enough noise to raise the dead.

"Graceful," Lloyd commented as he swept into the kitchen behind me.

He surveyed the room in sweeping motions with his rifle aimed and ready for any threat. That's probably the way I should have entered the house, instead of my spastic pirouetting ballerina move that had left me with a bruised hip and an even more bruised ego. "Whatever," I muttered as I fought against the urge to rub my hip.

Bret and Jenna entered with the same reserve and caution that Lloyd had exhibited. Bret shook his head at me, his disapproval and censure obvious. Jenna didn't look at me as she eagerly scanned the kitchen. She lowered the pistol she had been holding and raced from the room.

"Jenna wait!" Bret ordered but she had already disappeared from view.

"Mom! Dad! Aunt Lucy!" her cries became distant as she disappeared into the bowels of the house.

Lloyd nodded to Bret. "Follow her. We'll check out the lower floor." He turned to me. "You going to actually get your gun ready?"

I glared at him, but took his advice and pulled my rifle forward as Bret disappeared. We swept through the rooms rapidly as we searched for anything out of place, but there was nothing. Absolutely nothing. A soft thump sounded from above. I tilted my head back, holding my breath as I stared at the ceiling expectantly. No shouts rang out but I could make out the sound of their footfalls as they moved across one of the rooms.

"Did anything even happen on this street or did they all take off? Did they somehow escape The Freezing?" I whispered.

Lloyd didn't look at me as he fondled the brown stalks of a spider plant between his fingers. The baby offshoots had already fallen off and dropped to the floor. There was a look on his face that left me breathless and aching for things forever lost to us.

"I don't know," he murmured.

"None of this seems right. It's like we're trapped in an alternate universe, we're the ones stuck on the side where there's no one left. The other side is still moving, still alive and they either don't remember that we existed, or they're baffled by the sudden disappearance of so many."

"I had one of these plants as a child. I would have taken it to boot camp but they wouldn't let me. I don't know what became of it." Or his family, I heard the unspoken words even though he didn't say them. I had to blink back the tears that burned my eyes as I sensed his grief. Lloyd cocked one reddish eyebrow at me as he finally released the plant and turned toward me. "An alternate universe, huh?"

"Or something like that," I managed to choke out.

"It's nothing like that," he said. "Jenna is still moving; it only makes sense her aunt would be the same way. There is no alternate universe here, only lucky people, and the highly unlucky."

"Which side do we fall on?" I inquired dryly.

He grinned at me, but the smile didn't reach his eyes. "I haven't decided yet, graceful." Though I tried not to, I couldn't help but grin back at him. "This *is* a creepy road though."

"Whole damn town has been creepy so far."

"It has," he agreed, idly turning his attention back to the plant.

I left him to his memories. I needed a moment to gather my thoughts, and regain some of my courage. I could feel it waning in this strange land of seemingly utter calm and tranquility. I knew better than to think that things were just as they seemed. I couldn't help but think we'd just stepped straight into the spider's web and that it was just waiting to spin us into a cocoon and drain us dry.

I walked back into the kitchen. Barney was lying on the floor, his front paws crossed before him, and his head resting on them. He cocked one ear and opened one eye to watch as I walked around the room. I opened cabinets, looking for food but looking more for a distraction from my thoughts. They seemed to have been completely picked over. Someone had survived The Freezing, whether it was Jenna's aunt, her parents, or other survivors I didn't know, but the only thing left in the cabinet's were a box of baking soda and a thing of vanilla.

I closed the cabinet full of cleaning supplies and turned to the fridge. My eyes widened, my mouth dropped as I spotted the note stuck to the fridge by a magnet picturing Jenna sitting on Santa's lap. The picture was a good ten years old, but I had known her then, and the strawberry colored pigtails and dazzling smile were instantly recognizable. I tore the note from the fridge. I wanted to read it, to know what it said, but it wasn't my note and I couldn't bring myself to know about Jenna's family before she did.

I nearly ran from the room as I searched Jenna out. I glanced into the room where I had left Lloyd. He was standing by the window, his hands clasped behind him as he lifted his face to the sun. His eyes were closed as he appeared to find some solace in the warm rays. There was something peaceful and almost joyous about him. I took comfort in the small moment of pleasure he seemed to have found.

I tore my attention away, I had to find Jenna, and I was unwilling to interrupt Lloyd. I tried to be quiet in my excited rush as I hurried up the stairs. I hit the top of the stairs, and turned the corner to find Bret standing in a doorway. His eyes were sad as they landed on me, his mouth drawn into a flat line. I froze, uncertain what to do, I held either joy or a major letdown within my grasp. I wished that I *had* read the note because judging by the look on Bret's face, whatever was in that room was *not* good.

Bret frowned at me; his eyes flitted down to my now fisted hand. He glanced back into the room before breaking away and coming to join me. "What is it?" he asked in a low voice.

I looked behind him, but Jenna was nowhere to be seen. "I found a note with Jenna's name on it."

"What does it say?"

I shook my head as I licked my lips nervously. "I didn't read it, it's not my note. What's going on?"

"It's her aunt, she's frozen."

Disappointment for Jenna filled me, but there was also something else that buzzed around at the back of my mind like an annoying gnat on a hot summer day. Something was *wrong*. I buried the niggling doubt beneath the returning hope that what I held was good news. *Some*one had left the note for her. "She has to see this."

Bret nodded as he turned away from me. He hesitated and took a deep breath before he stepped through the bedroom doorway to speak with Jenna. Lloyd had crept up the stairs so soundlessly that I didn't know he was there until he stepped onto the landing behind me. I lifted the note for him to see, but he didn't ask any questions, and I didn't offer any information as Jenna emerged from the room. Her eyes were red rimmed, her face streaked with the tears that had slipped down her pale cheeks.

I held my breath as I handed the note out to her. *It has to be good news; it has to be good news*. Jenna frowned at me but slipped the now crumpled paper from my grasp and pulled it open.

"It's from my mom," she breathed.

I inhaled a shaky breath as hope tore through me. Jenna's face lit with the pure joy of a six year old on Christmas morning and her striking green eyes shone with tears of happiness. "They're alive, they *both* are. Or at least they were a week ago. She says they waited for me for a week, but there were other survivors moving through and they realized they had to move on also. They're heading into Boston, in the hope that there will be more survivors and protection there. She's not sure exactly where they will be. No matter what, as long as one of them is still alive, they will leave me a note either at my grandmother's house, the science museum, Paul Revere's house, or in a mailbox at a home on Beacon Hill. She says they love me and miss me. There are tear marks on the paper."

Jenna was also crying by the time she was done giving us the details of the note. I didn't think she realized this though as she was smiling radiantly and didn't wipe the tears from her face. "Why so many places?" Bret asked.

"In case one or all of the others are destroyed," Lloyd answered. "Or in case they don't make it near any of the others."

"They will go to my grandmother's, no matter what," Jenna insisted.

"But there is no guarantee your grandmother's house will be standing."

Though the words were harsh and clipped, Jenna didn't flinch from the truth of them. "It's ok, they're *alive*," she breathed. "I'll find them, no matter what, and that is all that matters."

I nodded my agreement. She had come this far, her parents had come this far, I firmly believed they would be reunited again, and I was going to do everything I could to make that happen. "I should have left a note," Bret mumbled.

I rested my hand on his arm and squeezed it comfortingly. "You couldn't have known that your mother probably wasn't affected."

"I still should have done it; I just assumed that we would be able to get back…"

His voice trailed off, his strong jaw clenched as he turned away from me. I could sense his suffering and frustration, even though he was trying to keep it buried. "There are plenty of us that wish we could have done things differently, unfortunately there is no changing the past. We have each other, we have our lives, and we have to keep moving forward," Lloyd said briskly.

I didn't ask what had happened to his family; he probably didn't know and none of us liked to be reminded of the loved ones we'd lost. "There's always hope," I whispered, briefly recalling my dream of Cade earlier.

Bret's forest colored, beautiful green eyes came back to me. For one brief, highly alarming minute, I saw only despair in a gaze that had always been so full of happiness. Then, much to my relief, he managed a small smile and squeezed my hand. "Yes, there is."

I realized too late that he might have taken my words the wrong way. That he may think that I meant hope for him and me again, when that was the last thing in the world I'd meant. I glanced nervously at Jenna; I didn't want her to think I had changed my mind about Bret. We'd just become tenuous friends, I didn't want to ruin that, but she was still staring in astonishment at the paper in her hands. I jumped a little when Bret's thumb slid over my hand.

"Your parents may still be out there, there is a chance you will see them again," I elaborated as I gently pulled my hand away from Bret's. "At least we know there were other survivors that moved through this town."

"And we had better get moving too," Lloyd said. "If we intend to get to the hospital before sunset."

"Just let me say goodbye to my aunt," Jenna spun on her heel.

"Who?" Lloyd asked in surprise.

"Her aunt. She's frozen," I explained.

"*What* is she!?" Lloyd's eyes looked like they were about to bug out of his head like some crazy cartoon character.

I glanced nervously at Bret, thinking that Lloyd had flipped, that perhaps something in his mind had finally cracked. Lloyd knew about The Frozen Ones, we had done nothing but encounter them for the past month. They had been nearly impossible to avoid, in the beginning, if we moved further than five feet at a time. How could Lloyd possibly have forgotten about that, and why was he looking at me as if he was about to strangle the life from me?

I took a hasty step back. I'd become more competent with weapons, and fighting over the past few weeks, but I did *not* want to take on a man that had been highly trained by the army. "*What* is she!?" Lloyd demanded again, but this time his voice was low and gravelly.

"She's frozen, you know...one of them," Bret said slowly obviously as distrustful of Lloyd's strange reaction as I was.

Lloyd let loose with a flurry of curses that would have caused even the most seasoned truck driver to blush. They sure made me gape, and even question what a few of the things he said meant. "We need to go!" he declared forcefully at the end.

"We're going in a moment," Bret told him.

"No! Now! We have to go *now*!"

Lloyd shoved roughly past me and stormed down the hall at a rapid pace that left Bret and I staring after him in disbelief. "What was *that*?" I whispered.

"No idea," Bret responded as he shook his head. "Let's hope our trained killer hasn't flipped his lid though."

"Bret..."

My words were cut off as Jenna began to protest vehemently from the bedroom. Lloyd ignored her protests as he began to drag her down the hall toward us. "Move out!" he snapped.

"Lloyd what is going on?" I demanded. I was unwilling to go anywhere with him until I knew where his sudden, and seemingly irrational, fear had come from.

"We can talk as we move. Now *move!*"

I was more frightened by the look in his eyes than by his behavior. He was speaking like he was angry, like he was on the verge of shattering completely, but there was pure terror blazing from his eyes. I fled down the stairs, Bret followed close behind and Jenna had stopped protesting by the time I made it to the bottom floor.

I rushed into the kitchen, realizing only belatedly that I had been too distracted by the note to check inside the fridge. I didn't think there was much hope for anything in there, but it was worth a peek. I flung the door open and froze. The power hadn't gone out in this area of town so some of the food had managed to stay good, but there was green ooze seeping from the crisper and a fetid odor assaulted me. There were also two boxes of Cheerios, one of Special K, and a Raisin Bran sitting on the shelf amongst the mess. In front of them was a post-it that read 'Jenna'.

"Thank you Mr. and Mrs. Howe." I didn't know why her parents had placed them in the fridge, perhaps they'd hoped to keep them fresher, but I didn't care. I swung my backpack forward and began to shove the boxes inside as the other three entered the room.

"Bethany," Lloyd hissed.

"One minute," I retorted as I shoved the third box into my bag. It wasn't going to zip all the way closed again, but I didn't care. The cereal would keep us going for a few more days, maybe even a week or more if we were careful with it.

"Bethany let's go!"

I tried to pull my arm from Lloyd's iron tight grasp. Though he was thin, he was far stronger than he appeared as he clung to me. "The cereal!" I cried.

He shoved his face into mine. "Screw the cereal!" he snarled.

I blinked in astonishment as he threw my bag onto my back. The last box of Cheerios fell to the floor. Barney had already been on his feet, but now he surged eagerly forward as the little O's scattered across the linoleum. "Wait!" I gasped as I was pulled roughly forward. "Barney."

Lloyd wasn't listening to me though as he drug me toward where Jenna and Bret waited by the door. Jenna looked anxious; Bret just looked completely baffled by everything. "What is your problem!?" I demanded breathlessly.

"The aunt is frozen," Lloyd finally responded with something more than a command.

"So are a *lot* of other people," I retorted growing more concerned about his erratic behavior.

Lloyd glanced back at me. "She's frozen and she's still *here*. The rest of the town has been cleared out already."

The niggling feeling I'd experienced upstairs came flooding forth like water from a bursting dam. Though I hadn't quite understood what had been bothering me at the time, I understood it now, and I cursed myself for being an idiot. *Every* other place we had come across in this area had been damaged, and completely devoid of human beings. But not here, in this frozen Mayberry of peace and tranquility. No, here everything was still perfect, still as intact as it had been before the moment that had shattered our lives. Everything was as it had been; including the people that were unable to flee from the monsters that would seek them out in order to drain them of their life.

Monsters that would be heading *our* way.

"Crap," I breathed.

"Yes crap, now let's go."

I didn't protest anymore. I fled out the door and pounded down the steps of the porch. I turned back to call out to Barney as Bret and Jenna raced across the street toward the woods. My voice froze in my throat though as I realized that everything had gone deathly silent once again. My terrified gaze swung to Lloyd, I saw the answering panic in his eyes.

Barney emerged onto the porch, his ears pricked and his nose raised to the wind. The hair on the back of his neck stood up seconds before one of the monstrous things rose up from behind the house. It wasn't as large as the house, or at least its main bulk wasn't, but this one had become big enough so that one of the tentacles was able to reach the second story windows. It was only that tentacle I saw at first, as the rest of it was blocked by the home.

Its opalescent and red bulge began to squish and push its way in between Jenna's aunt's house and her neighbor's. Boards were ripped free, windows shattered, the front porch beams splintered like toothpicks beneath the weight of the bulging creature pressing upon it. That thing was what had caused the antique store my mother had died in to collapse. That thing was what had ripped the roof of the antique building free and broken bracings with seeming ease.

Its progress was hindered by its size, but that wasn't going to stop it as part of the house gave way to its heavy bulk. It seemed that as long as the atrocities continued to consume blood, they also continued to grow in both width and height.

Barney leapt off the porch as one of the tentacles whipped toward him. He let out a startled yelp as he barely managing to avoid the things hungry grasp. "Barney," I whispered as I slid to a stop.

"It's a dog!" Lloyd shouted. "And he's faster than *you*!"

I was torn between going back for the dog, and listening to the complete and utter logic that Lloyd shouted. In the end, it was Barney's speed and cunning ability to avoid the whipping tentacles that made sane reasoning finally return. The dog bounded forward with grace and speed. He nearly beat *me* into the relative safety of the woods.

I plunged into the forest at the same time that three more of the monsters emerged onto the street. Two of them came straight at us.

CHAPTER 7

"Zigzag," Lloyd ordered.

He didn't have to tell me twice as I raced in and out of the trees. I didn't know what good it was going to do us though, those things were fast, and their freaking tentacles were even faster. We had no position to stand and fight, not right now anyway. We needed higher ground, but the last thing I was going to do was climb a tree. I'd never survive then, a tree was no obstacle for them.

Unfortunately there appeared to be no other high ground around us. My gaze searched wildly around the forest, looking for something, *anything* that would give us some sort of protection or shelter. I glanced over my shoulder, Jenna was already starting to lag a little, and I could feel the burn in my lungs and legs. We couldn't keep this up for much longer, and judging by the rapid snapping of trees resonating behind us, we weren't putting much ground between us and them.

Lloyd jumped onto a set of boulders; he turned partially around to survey the woods. He leapt off the boulders and disappeared briefly from view. I pushed myself to keep going, but the backpack was becoming steadily heavier, and my legs hurt more and more with every step I took.

Barney brushed briefly against my legs before moving ahead. The saying that a person didn't have to be the fastest in the group when being chased, they just had to be fastest than the slowest member, flashed through my mind. Apparently Barney knew this saying, and lived by it. Then again, Bret was staying behind me and though I couldn't see her, I knew that Jenna was falling even further behind.

Maybe some people wouldn't mind just being able to beat someone in order to survive, but I did. There was no way I was going to allow Jenna to be lost, not like this anyway, and I certainly wasn't going to lose Bret. There had to be something that we could do. Even if those things did catch Jenna, they weren't going to stop with just her anyway. They would take us all down one by one.

Lloyd suddenly reappeared, he was standing on another set of boulders, his rifle raised, his eye pressed to the scope. The boom of the shot was startling in the forest but no birds took flight.

Where did they all go when they felt the approach of these things?

I suddenly, and uselessly, wished for wings too. Though I didn't think there was any chance he could hit one of them through the trees, Lloyd fired off another shot. He probably just hoped to make them hesitate; I didn't think for one minute that it would work.

I leapt onto the boulder beside Lloyd and struggled to catch my breath as I studied the forest. I could see trees bending and hear them fracture, but I couldn't see the monsters causing it through the thick foliage of the trees. I may not be able to see them yet, but they were noticeably closer.

"Keep going." Lloyd was annoyingly less out of breath than me and my rapid panting.

"We have to make a stand."

Lloyd barely glanced at me before firing off another round. "Do you honestly think we can beat those things?"

"Do you honestly think we can outrun them?" I managed to choke out, horrified by the notion that Lloyd didn't think we could beat them.

"Run."

"Don't wait too long."

I jumped off the boulder and fled into the woods behind Jenna and Bret now. We had to find somewhere to go to ground or we were going to die. My heart pounded, I could hear the blood rushing through my ears in giant pulsing waves. My vision was beginning to blur as I labored to breathe.

Hope, I was trying to cling to some hope, but it was completely eluding me right now. All I had was mind numbing fear.

I was so focused on keeping my legs moving, and trying to see through the bright stars exploding before my eyes, that I didn't realize Bret and Jenna had stopped until I nearly plowed into them. "Who the hell puts a fence in the middle of the freaking forest!?" Bret exploded.

Horror filled me, my mouth dropped as I stared at the chain link fence before us with barbwire twisted thickly around the top of it. I looked to the right, then to the left, but the fence stretched as far as I could see. A strange guttural sound escaped me.

"This way," Bret said crisply.

He turned to the right and began to run along the length of the fence. I didn't know what he was looking for, but he kept his hand on the fence as he moved. I glanced over my shoulder and relief filled me as I caught sight of Lloyd closing in on us. Bret hugged the fence line, but it was Barney that found the hole first. I didn't even see it, or know that we had gone past it, until I realized Barney was on the other side.

"We missed something!" I gasped.

Barney followed me as I dashed back along the fence. "Bethany!" Bret growled.

Though Barney didn't bark, he began to run back and forth in the same area. I tried to push myself harder, but my legs were too tired, and I was too fatigued to move any faster than I already was. I skidded to a halt, nearly falling over as I stopped abruptly. Barney's tail wagged in eager excitement as he made one more trip back and forth. Vines and weeds had encroached on both sides of the fence. It was easy to see how we had missed the hole even though it was a decent size.

"Here!" I called. "Here!"

The bittersweet and grape vine cut into my hands and tore at my skin as I yanked at it, but it stuck to the fence with frustrating tenacity. Lloyd appeared at my side, his eyes narrowed as he pulled and ripped at the vines with me. "Go," he ordered when we had cleared enough of the hole to fit through. "Go Bethany!"

I slid into the hole and tugged at my shirt as it snagged on a piece of broken metal. I heard my shirt tear, felt the bite of metal against my back, but I didn't care. I pushed Barney back as he eagerly tried to lick my face. "They should have named you Lassie," I muttered at him.

He licked me one more time before backing away. His tail tucked between his legs, his ass end dropped down as he began to cower. I refused to look behind me, refused to see what had him so frightened and what he could see approaching but I couldn't.

Jenna, Bret, and Lloyd came through the fence next. "This way," Lloyd said.

Lloyd broke into a brisk run that we all labored to keep up with. Though the fence had kept us out, there was no doubt that it would do the same for the things hunting us. "Wait!" I called as I skidded to a halt.

"What is it?" Jenna demanded.

"Shh," I whispered and placed my finger against my lips as I watched Barney. His withers were hunched up and his head tilted to the sky. If I concentrated I could hear a low humming noise disturbing the air. I frowned as I turned my attention to the sky. The ships had always been nearly noiseless; I'd never heard them so clearly before, not even when they'd been directly overhead. However, I was certain they were there now, coming toward us, searching for us. *Hunting* us.

"Against the trees!" I commanded. "Now! Against the trees! Against the trees!"

They looked at me like I was speaking Russian but followed my lead as I flattened myself against the tree. My back pressed against the trunk, my arms wrapped around it. I silently cursed the scraggly pines that sprouted everywhere throughout Plymouth and offered little shelter. I would have cut off my own hand for a giant oak or maple tree right now. Even a Locust would be better. But all we had were the small rough trees and the little bit of protection they offered us.

I was trying not to shake, straining not to completely freak out and go fleeing through the woods as the rapid beat of my heart echoed in my ears. Especially as the sound of breaking trees continued to ring through the air and one of those things steadily grew closer. We were trapped, cornered beneath what was hunting us from above, and what was pursuing us from on the ground.

"What do we do?" Jenna whispered.

We all looked to Lloyd, but he seemed just as confused and uncertain as I was. What could we do? If we continued to run the ship would only track us from above. It would follow us through the woods, and none of us knew exactly what their defensive mechanisms were capable of. I thought of the bridge from when we had been escaping Cape Cod, of the blinding white light that had erupted from nowhere. I recalled Aiden's description of the man, the one that had seemed to burn from the inside out. The one who'd had flames shoot from his mouth seconds before becoming a crumbling pile of ash. The heat it had taken to incinerate a person so completely, in such a short time was nothing short of amazing, and terrifying.

Though the ships hadn't been present at the bridge, there was no way to know if perhaps they had the capability of doing such a thing also. My fingernails came up with rough hewn bark and sap as they dug into the tree. *Not now, not like this.* I couldn't go out like this. I was shaking, trembling so fiercely I was certain my legs were going to give out.

It seemed as if a solar eclipse was beginning to take over the sun as the shadows lengthened across the ground and the day became dusk in a matter of seconds. Then something straight out of a horror movie slid into view. It took over our world and encompassed everything above us. Barney cowered by my side with his head down and his ears flattened against his skull.

I don't know why he stayed with me, why he didn't just run. He had a chance of escaping these things. He was faster than us, and they might not even want a dog. But then again I didn't think they would discriminate against anything warm blooded, or cold, for that matter.

I tilted my head back as the ship crept over us. The sun's rays shone around the edges of it, but the dusk of the day was absolute with the massive ship above us. Barney whimpered as he pressed against my wobbling legs.

A loud thump echoed through the forest that caused me to tear my eyes away from the ship as the beasts appeared to be moving away. We had managed to elude them for now, and they appeared to have lost our trail, but it wouldn't stay that way if that ship spotted us.

I didn't know if the ships had spotlights but I felt as if one was shining down on us, trying to locate us amongst the trees. I could hear Jenna's rapid pants and her eyes were shooting all over the place. Bret remained motionless against the tree next to her. Lloyd was the only one with his weapon held firmly before him. His hand pressed over the glass of the scope as he watched the tree line.

I took a deep breath, closed my eyes and bowed my head. I needed a moment to draw upon the courage I felt rapidly slipping away. *Just breathe*, I told myself over and over again. *Just breathe.*

Heat washed over me. I opened my eyes and blinked against the sudden influx of light against my irises. I was briefly convinced that it was the same blinding light that had burnt the others alive. A strangled cry escaped me as I realized the sun was no longer blocked out. The ship was still visible over the tops of the trees, but it had moved on to scan another area of the forest, leaving behind its monsters to scour for us.

"They're going to try and box us in," Lloyd muttered. "Move parallel to each other and squeeze us together. They'll eventually pin us in."

"What do we do?" Jenna breathed.

Lloyd glanced rapidly around and then heaved a big sigh. "You're not going to like it."

"Just tell us," Bret said impatiently.

"We double back."

My mouth dropped as my head turned toward where we had just come from. "But there are even *more* of them back there!" I hissed.

"They don't expect us to go back that way though. They think we're still running, still heading north. They're going to move that way for awhile, and eventually they're going to realize that we're not there. They're going to assume that we found a place to hide and come back this way. They won't expect us to go back toward their other monsters."

"Lloyd..."

"I told you that you wouldn't like it. If we keep going this way they're eventually going to squeeze us. If we go back we may be able to skirt them completely. We're going to lose time, but it's the only way."

The snapping treetops were a good two hundred yards away, but Lloyd was right, they *were* narrowing in on a point further ahead. A point they expected us to be at, as did the ship. I shuddered and a shard of bark slid beneath my fingernail. It was only that, and the aching pain in my arms, that caused me to realize I was still clinging to the tree. I released it and dropped my deadened arms back to my side.

I rubbed my wrists tiredly; my gaze scoured the forest for some escape other than what Lloyd was suggesting. "Can we stay behind them and follow them out of here?" Jenna asked.

"Once they meet up and realize they haven't trapped us they're probably going to double back."

"But we're going back that way too," Bret pointed out.

"Not if we can cut across somehow, get back to an area they've already been through. We have to get away from them and make our way to the hospital," Lloyd said.

"That's a big if."

"If we stay here we die, and that's a *definite* if."

I slid down the tree to sit and recoup some of my waning strength and energy. "We should rest for five minutes, eat quickly, and then go," I suggested. "We're not going to have many other opportunities and we need the energy boost."

"Oh God," Jenna's hands flew to her throat. "I'm sorry this is all my fault. I'm so sorry."

Bret draped his arm around her shoulders in an effort to soothe her. "It's no one's fault, we all agreed to this." My growing sense of urgency made my tone brisker than I'd intended.

I pulled my backpack forward and tugged out a box of Cheerios. Making a bowl with my dirty t-shirt I dumped some into it. There was a time when I would have balked against eating from something so dirty, now I gave it no further thought. I placed a couple handfuls on the ground for Barney who eagerly accepted the meager meal. I rubbed his ear as I passed the box to Jenna.

CHAPTER 8

It was nearly impossible to see once night arrived. Thunder clouds had begun to roll in around sunset and they now blocked out whatever illumination the moon might have provided. Out of habit I had been squinting to see through the gloom, but I'd stopped when I realized I was able to make out far more details than I had expected in the shifting shadows. Apparently we'd been spending so much time moving at night that my eyes had become accustomed and adjusted to it.

Apparently I'd also become more adapt at moving through the woods. I wondered briefly if Darnell's training, and the fact that we had been living like forest creatures for the past month had finally helped to break me of some of my clumsiness. Either way, I'd only tripped a few times and miraculously hadn't fallen all the way down yet. Lloyd pulled out the map, consulted it briefly, and slid it back into his belt. We'd been walking for hours but I had no idea where we were, not anymore. By now my blisters had blisters and they were all irritated and sore.

"We're almost back to the main part of town; we can cross under cover of darkness and hopefully be back at the state forest by sunrise," Lloyd told us.

The last thing I wanted was to go back through that ghost town again but I kept my thoughts to myself. We were all scared, voicing my fears wasn't going to help us any. I kept my attention focused on my feet as I tried to stay as quiet as possible. The solid wall of a tree knocked me back when my right shoulder connected with it.

Lloyd shot me a cross look as I uttered a muffled curse and rubbed my offended shoulder. The tree shook from the impact and the leaves rustled within the bowers. Bret was biting his lip as he tried not to laugh, Jenna was staring at me incredulously, and even Barney looked as if he thought

I was an idiot as he cocked one ear at me. Bret took hold of my hand, I tried to tug it free but he held it firmly within his grasp.

"Haven't seen that yet tonight," he said.

"Seen what?" I muttered, angered and embarrassed by what had just occurred. I'd been doing so well tonight, but apparently my clumsiness was more ingrained than I'd realized.

"Your inherent grace." I scowled at him. "You watch your feet and I'll watch the trees."

I couldn't argue with that as he led me through the forest. I was ok with keeping my head down anyway, there wasn't much I would like to see right now. In all honesty I thought that if he led the way I might actually fall asleep for a bit while walking. Though I doubted that was possible, I was exhausted enough to try it and find out.

My mind went blank, I zoned out as we moved. I was too tired to think about anything other than putting one foot in front of the other. I was pretty sure I was nearly asleep when Bret stopped moving and I walked right into him. "Sorry," I mumbled as he righted me.

"It's ok."

I blinked rapidly, trying to clear my blurry vision and the sleepiness clinging to me. I shuddered involuntarily and couldn't stop myself from taking a hasty step back as I realized we were back at the main road. The buildings, or what remained of the buildings, sprawled out before us. It reminded me of the pictures of old ghost towns I'd seen. All it needed was tumbleweed rolling down the street and the creepiness of this town would be complete.

"We stay low and we move fast." Lloyd checked his gun as he spoke the words. His jaw was clenched, his gaze relentless as he turned his attention to me. Beneath his toughened exterior I could sense his trepidation. "We've made it this far."

What he didn't say, but I already knew, was that we were lucky to have made it this far. But how long could our luck hold out for? How long could we keep going on fumes and chance?

I double checked my gun too; more to distract myself from my thoughts than with any real concern that there was something wrong with it. "Keep a close eye on that dog; he's our best indicator of any threat."

"Barney." I said more out of habit then with any real hope that Lloyd might start calling him something other than *that dog*.

Lloyd didn't respond as he slipped from the shadows of the woods and hit the street. We stayed close on his heels as we dashed down the street far faster than we had moved down it last time. In the darkness it was tough to see the debris that littered the way, but I was able to avoid most of it by following Barney.

I could scarcely breathe, my heart was hammering, but my feet continued to move forward and so far we were all still alive. So far. It wasn't that hot out but sweat was running down my face and into my eyes. I had to juggle my gun in order to wipe my brow with the back of my arm.

I wanted to go to sleep tonight and wake up in my bed, in my room, in my home, with my siblings and my mother. I wanted Cade.

I was so filled with a desperate need for all of this to not be real that I almost sat down on the sidewalk and lost myself to the memories and despair engulfing me. I grit my teeth as I fought against the waves of melancholy that threatened to consume me. This was not the place, and this was *not* the time to completely lose control. In fact, there *was* no time for thoughts like the ones I was having. Not anymore. Not if I planned to keep my sanity and retain any measure of hope.

There was only time for survival in this world, and we *had* to survive.

I forced myself to take deep breaths in an attempt to get air back into my burning lungs. "What *is* that?"

I turned, expecting Jenna to be right behind me, but she had stopped moving and had fallen a little behind us. I stopped and pressed myself against the cool brick of a nearby building as I searched for whatever it was that she was talking about. "What's what?" Bret inquired.

Though it was gloomy I could make out the frown that marred Jenna's pretty features. I just couldn't see what was causing it. I partially stepped away from the building to search the area that she was staring at, but I saw nothing. "Let's go!" Lloyd barked.

"Jenna what is it?" I asked.

She shook her head and jogged toward us. "Never mind, it must have been nothing."

Barney remained by my side, but he seemed unfazed as he lay down and rested his head on his paws. He wouldn't be so relaxed if there was something out there. But there was one thing I had learned over the past month, it was *never* just nothing. "We have to go," I told her.

I wanted off of this street and out of this godforsaken town. Lloyd darted across a side road. He was momentarily exposed before he reached the other side and plastered himself against the building. Bret bolted across next, with Barney following behind him at a leisurely jog. I was about to follow after them when I heard Jenna mutter something.

I took a step forward at the same time that I turned toward her. The uncoordinated move almost caused me to fall on my ass as I stepped off the curb. I managed to keep myself upright by falling against the building. Aggravation spurted through me as I shoved off the cool brick façade.

"Jenna!" I snarled.

She was moving away from me, creeping back the way we had come. *What was she doing?* I wondered, *was she trying to get us all killed?*.

"Hello," her call was soft, but it caused the hair on the nape of my neck to stand on end and my heart to plummet into my stomach. We had labored to stay as silent as possible and now she was calling out into the night as if it were the safest thing in the world to do.

"Jenna!" Her name barely escaped my lips but I knew that she could hear me.

"There's someone…"

Goose pimples broke out on my body as the sweat coating me turned to ice. A shiver slid down my spine, as an intense fear began to take a firm hold of my entire body. I wasn't sure if I was going to scream at her or run away.

Before I fully registered what I was going to do, I was already doing it.

I bolted into the street and ran for Jenna who was already a good hundred feet away from me. She took a step closer to the road, her attention fixated on something across the street. I was finally able to see what had captivated her so completely that she seemed to have forgotten all sense of self preservation. My legs nearly gave out as I spotted the slender boy standing within the shadows of the buildings on the other side of the road.

Time seemed to slow as everything became as crisp and clear as an early winter morning on the beach. I could make out every detail of the objects within the night; clearly see every different strand of color within Jenna's red hued hair. The lack of light was no longer a problem as I recognized the certain death lurking within the shadows. It was a disconcerting feeling, one that left me shaken, but it didn't stop my onward rush as my legs pumped faster than I'd ever thought possible.

Jenna stepped off the curb and into the street. I clearly recalled the young girl that had killed Sarah. The young girl that had seemed so real and vulnerable yet harbored a hideous monster, a girl that Jenna had been told about, but had not actually *seen* with her own eyes.

"We can help you!" Jenna quietly called.

"No Jenna!" I gasped.

My adrenaline fueled mind was oblivious of the jeopardy it was in as I flung myself off the sidewalk at Jenna. The body of the young boy unraveled in the blink of an eye to reveal the hideous fiend hidden just beneath the surface. One of those awful tentacles whipped out with the amazing speed and deadly accuracy of a cheetah.

I hit Jenna with the full force of my body. Knocking her off balance, I shoved her out of the way of the deadly attack seconds before the tentacle would have demolished her chest. I stumbled, nearly fell, but the thing slammed into my shoulder. It knocked me back as the tentacle pierced my body.

A scream rose up my throat but came out as garbled nonsense. Bone or cartilage snapped like a firecracker as it was bent in a direction it was never meant to go. White stars exploded before my eyes as I was pushed back beneath the force of the creature. I expected to feel the rough impact of the road against my back, but it didn't come as the tentacle dug into my shoulder and lifted me above the ground.

I attempted to raise my hands to grasp hold of the thing torturing me. My arms were like lead weights though as they hung limply at my sides. I didn't have time to worry that I was going to die. I was too caught up in the pain enshrouding me, wrapping around me, and freezing me within its deadly grasp. A high pitched ringing exploded in my ears, filling everything that I was with its intense noise. I thought that it might be my own screams I was hearing, but my voice was still trapped within me.

This was it; this was the way it was all going to end. I didn't find peace in that thought, my life didn't flash before my eyes, and I didn't feel terror. All I could see was the intense lights popping before me. I felt as if I were being ripped apart from the inside out; felt as if I were being flayed alive and stripped to the very bone. I felt as if I were being wrapped within a spider's cocoon, and encased to the point that motion and sound were no longer possible as the spider drained me of my blood.

My release came so suddenly that I didn't even recognize it for what it was, even as I tumbled to the ground. The unforgiving asphalt felt like a soft cushion after what I had just experienced. The piercing pop of gunshots reverberated in my ears, causing me to wince as normal sound blazed back into my tortured ears. I rolled over, tried to get up but found that my wobbly legs wouldn't support my weight.

"Grab her!" I heard Lloyd shout over the raining clatter of gunfire.

Hands grabbed my good arm as the other one hung uselessly against my side. "I'm sorry about this."

Before I could question what Bret was sorry for, he heaved me up and tossed me over his shoulder. I groaned as my wounded shoulder protested the movement, but it was still nothing compared to what I'd just endured. I bit my bottom lip hard enough to draw blood, but I didn't wince at the fleeting sting. Bret broke into a brisk jog as he hurried down the street with me hanging off his shoulder like a limp dishrag.

"The gunfire will draw them here. We have to get away. Now," Lloyd commanded.

I couldn't see him as I bounced against Bret's back, but his boots came into view as he crossed the road behind Bret. I could feel pain, normal pain, stealing through my body. My shoulder was pulsating and there was blood seeping down my arm. I knew that it was dripping off of me, but I couldn't see it landing on the street. The shock was gradually wearing off and I was beginning to realize that I was now a huge liability to them.

Not only was I dead weight, but I was also easily tracked.

"Bret put me down," I managed to mutter as we plummeted into the woods. "Bret…"

"You can't walk."

"I'm bleeding all over the place, they'll find us."

Lloyd's boots reappeared beneath my bouncing head. I could barely see through the jarring impact that every step caused. "Stop," Lloyd commanded. I felt his hands upon me as he helped to lift me from Bret's back. "We have to staunch the blood flow."

I felt somewhat dizzy, the world blurred before me as they lowered me to the ground. Jenna was gawking in horror as Lloyd pulled the sleeve of my shirt down to bare my exposed collarbone. I strained to see the injury, and then regretted it instantly. It was a disgusting, gaping mess of mottled flesh, bone, and blood. Even in the dark I could see the bruising that marred my skin and was spreading across my chest and arm. My blue veins were clearly visible against my unnaturally pale skin.

"The shoulder's dislocated," Lloyd mumbled. "We have to get it back into place before we can cauterize the wound."

"Before we *what*?" Bret demanded as my mouth dropped open.

I tried to squirm away from them but my strength was waning, my head was spinning, and I wasn't sure I had the strength to fight off a gnat right now. Lloyd gave Bret a stern look before shaking his head. "It's the only way," he muttered.

"Stitches..."

"Do you have a needle and thread?" Lloyd demanded. His jaw was clenched and it was obvious that he didn't want to do this either, but he *would* if he had to.

"What about infection?"

"Penicillin..."

"Allergic," I managed to grate out between my suddenly chattering teeth.

"Good to know." Lloyd dug into his pack and rooted around as he searched for something. "We'll find something for you, but we can't wait to stitch it. They'll track that blood…"

"I know." I was trying to sound brave, but my weak tone and trembling body gave me away. "Fine... I'll be... fine."

"Are you cold?" Jenna demanded as she knelt by my side.

"She's in shock." Lloyd turned back to me, and though his face was relentless there was unease in his sky colored eyes. "And if we don't stop the flow…"

"I'm sorry, I'm so sorry," Jenna gushed. "You told me, you *all* told me, but he just looked so real, so *helpless*. I really am sorry Bethy, if I had known…"

"It's ok," I chattered out unable to stand her guilt. "Not your fault."

"But it is!" she gushed as she leaned closer to me.

"You have to move back." Lloyd shouldered Jenna out of the way as he knelt before me. "Bite on this." Before I could react he shoved a rag into my mouth. I choked and tried to spit it out but he held it firmly in place. "This is going to hurt like hell but you can*not* scream. The scent of your blood is already a big enough draw without adding a blood curdling scream to it. Bite Bethany."

After what I had just experienced with that *thing,* I was fairly certain that nothing could truly hurt me again. To be fair, if I'd been able to scream when it had a hold of me I would have shredded my vocal cords. I didn't know if I could keep back a cry now though. I stopped fighting against the gag, closed my eyes and bit down as Lloyd seized hold of my brutalized shoulder.

"What are you…?"

Bret's question was cut off as Lloyd jerked on my shoulder. A loud crack, much like a bat hitting a ball, split the air as my shoulder was wrenched back into place. I cried out against the gag, unable to keep the sound suppressed. Thankfully, the gag did. A wave of blackness washed over me as I teetered on the edge of passing out.

"Some warning would have been nice," Bret growled.

"There is no time for niceties," Lloyd retorted. My eyes rolled, I wanted the foul tasting gag out of my mouth but I knew that wasn't going to happen. Not yet anyway. "The shirt has to come off."

The last thing I was going to be able to do was lift my arm above my head. Bret started to protest but Lloyd brandished a knife and deftly slit the front of my shirt open. Bret's face flamed red as he hastily turned away, but Lloyd remained analytical and distant as he tugged the tattered remains of clothing from my beaten body.

There was a time when I would have been just as red as Bret, but not anymore. Now I didn't care that the only thing covering me was a bra, a bra that was white, tattered, and dirty. Modesty was something I didn't give much thought to anymore, and though I wasn't about to go wandering around nude, this bit of skin wasn't going to affect me even a little.

Lloyd's hand rested on my good shoulder, his gaze was fixed on me. I blinked as I tried to bring his face into focus. I was certain that I could take this, certain that I could take anything after the tremendous pain that *thing* had inflicted upon me. "Scream if you must. The rag will keep it muffled."

Lloyd turned away and pulled a long lighter from his bag. "What are you doing?" Jenna asked tremulously.

Lloyd didn't answer her as he tugged his belt off. I watched in wide eyed horror as he dug a small hole underneath a stone and built a quick fire beneath it. When the flame was a decent enough size and glowing red with heat, Lloyd placed the large belt buckle into it. The buckle was square and flat, but I was fairly certain that I'd once seen a horse engraved upon it. I was about to be branded by a freaking belt buckle, and tattooed with a horse. Or at least I hoped it was a horse, it may have been a camel for all I knew.

"Your belt buckle?" Bret demanded incredulously.

"Do you have anything else that's metal and big enough to cover that gash all at once, or would you like me to hold the lighter to her skin for awhile?"

All color vanished from Bret's face; he looked like he was going to be sick as he looked back at me. I was tempted to spit out the gag and stand up and run. How had my life become this messed up? All the technology and advancements I had grown up with were gone, and I was about to receive a medieval cauterization in the middle of the twenty first century. With a freaking *belt buckle* of all things!

It all seemed so impossible, so surreal. If it wasn't for the three people sitting around me, and the trail of blood I was leaving behind, I would have run. There was only so much a human being could take after all, and I was rapidly nearing my breaking point. But to run now was certain death. This had to happen or I would be hunted down and sucked dry before I could even make it a full mile.

A small trail of black smoke began to come off the belt buckle. It was taking on an ominous and glowing orange hue that caused bile to roll up my throat. Lloyd slipped his shirt off and wrapped it around his hand. It took me a minute to realize that he was going to grab hold of the buckle and press it to me. Dismay filled me as I realized this was going to burn him too, maybe not as bad, but he was going to be hurt. I closed my eyes, I couldn't watch anymore.

"I'm going to need you to hold her." There was no saliva left in my mouth as I tried to wet my parched throat. Bret's hands were kind as he grasped my good shoulder. "Not like a baby Bret, you need to hold her *still*," Lloyd said impatiently.

I didn't open my eyes, I refused to, but I knew the minute that the metal pressed against my skin. A garbled scream boiled up my throat, and froze there. The potent smell and sizzle of burned flesh drifted to me right before I passed out.

CHAPTER 9

It was nearing dawn when I awoke to a swaying motion that caused my stomach to heave violently. There were hands holding my calves, and another set grasping me under my armpits. I felt like a pig being led to the roast.

"You can put me down," I managed to croak out.

"You're awake." The relief in Bret's voice was palpable as his hands clenched upon me. I felt him bend over me as they stopped and his breath blew against my cheek. My eyelids fluttered open. It was disconcerting, and dizzying, as Bret appeared upside down over top of me.

"Please put me down."

They had stopped walking, and Lloyd lowered my feet to the ground as Bret supported my unsteady weight. I took stock of myself as I acknowledged all the aches in my overused, overworked, and beaten body. The burn high on my shoulder throbbed relentlessly. A hideous, puss filled blister had formed over it. I couldn't yet tell if it would eventually become a horse, or some other four legged creature.

My entire shoulder was an ugly mottled color of black and purple, but at least it wasn't bleeding anymore. The blood had been scrubbed from my body; I hated the fact that they had probably used some of our precious supply of water to do this. Someone, probably Bret as it seemed extra large, had taken a shirt and wrapped it around my chest. It was tied under my arms and knotted in the back by the sleeves.

"I was so worried."

Before I could react, before I even knew his intent, he bent and kissed me. I was so startled by the familiar comfort of his lips against mine that at first I didn't react. For a moment I was swept into a time when everything had been boring, safe, and secure. I was swept back to a time when I had been with Bret and content to stay that way, even with the lack of feeling and desire I'd felt for him. I had been willing to stay with Bret simply because I *did* love him and I cherished his friendship, even if he didn't cause my heart to race, didn't strengthen me, and love me unconditionally, and simply hadn't made me feel the way that Cade had.

His kiss swept me into a time before I had experienced the loss of everything I knew. A time before Cade, and the hole his death had left upon my tattered soul.

I wanted to stay this way, to forget and go back and never return to the stark reality of my loneliness and this cruel world. Never return to the hurt that hounded me constantly, even before the brutal assault I had just endured. But I couldn't. It wasn't fair to any of us if I did.

I pulled away, barely able to meet Bret's hopeful gaze as I shook my head at him. There was so much I should say to him, but the words caught in my throat. What could I say? I turned away from him and took a staggering step back. I felt weak, unsteady, but I was alive and that was all that mattered.

"Where are we?" I inquired groggily.

"Almost to the hospital," Lloyd answered." I turned toward him. Dirt and blood streaked his pale face; his nearly orange hair was standing on end. Shadows rimmed his bloodshot eyes and he was even paler than normal.

"You need a break," I said.

"We have to get to the hospital first. You need antibiotics, and we have to get this over and done with. There will be time to rest afterward."

"If you drop…"

"We've made it this far." It was the first time I noticed that Jenna was carrying my bag and gun as my attention was drawn to her. "It's not much further."

"I was out for a long time," I mumbled.

"You lost a lot of blood," Lloyd said.

I nodded absently as I gazed around the forest. It was thicker through here and there were more maples and oaks dotting the landscape. Even with the denser protection, I somehow felt more exposed. Maybe it was because I was injured, maybe it was because I had a shirt tied around me for clothing, or maybe it was simply because I resented my weakness.

"It's only another mile."

Lloyd was already walking again; I fell into step beside Jenna and stayed close by her side as I avoided Bret. I cursed my cowardice, but I had to avoid him right now. Jenna glanced at me, and I thought that she was going to say something, but she remained mute. Barney brushed against my legs as he danced around my feet.

We reached a small incline and climbed to the top of the hill. Beneath us the hospital spread out like some glittering mirage in the desert. The windows were ablaze in the gleam of the setting sun. It was oddly beautiful, and out of place, in the world surrounding us now.

Jenna's sky colored eyes gleamed as she grasped hold of my arm. "I didn't think we'd make it," she breathed.

I squeezed her hand. I didn't think any of us had thought we'd actually make it, but here we were, and there *it* was.

I was suddenly certain that something else was going to go wrong. Something far worse than the brutal assault, recently dislocated shoulder, and ugly blister I had endured. The three people with me seemed to feel the same as no one moved. They simply stared at the assortment of beautifully shining medical buildings.

"Should we wait till night?" I whispered.

"I don't think it matters," Lloyd answered.

"Let's just get this over with," Jenna said. "We've come so far."

I swallowed heavily and managed a small nod. "Yes, we have."

Lloyd cautiously began to make his way down the hill. Bret and Jenna followed him; I reluctantly took up the rear. My gun was strapped around me again, but the weight I had once found reassuring now seemed like a mere toy. I had seen what those things could do, but even more so I had *felt* the pain they were capable of inflicting. A pain that I could still feel tingling in the marrow of my bones and knew I would never forget. That agony hadn't been like having a sprained ankle or broken bone, or even a torn ligament, it was a memory that wouldn't fade with time and would haunt me for the rest of my days.

No wonder that man Cade and I had seen on the street (the only one we know to have been unfrozen), had been awakened by the brutal assault that the creature had inflicted upon him. Cade had attempted to awaken Peter, his old boss by burning him, but it had failed. I understood why now. The brand I sported on my shoulder was nothing compared to the engrained memory from when that thing had forced its way into my body. The people were frozen and could be awakened, but that kind of torment was something that we could never manage to inflict no matter how much we tried. Of that I was certain.

What I wasn't certain of was whether The Frozen Ones were dead or not. The man that had reawakened was proof that they had originally been alive, trapped within their own bodies, but that had been over a month ago. They may still be frozen, immobile statues, but they had to be dead by now.

Didn't they? They hadn't eaten, hadn't gone to the bathroom; hadn't even drawn a breath in so long. But could they somehow still be alive and possibly even aware of their surroundings?

I shuddered at the thought; goose bumps broke out on my flesh. The endless torture they were enduring if they were aware of their surroundings was a horror I couldn't even begin to fathom. I'd rather be dead.

I don't want to die.

The thought slammed into me. For the first time I realized that it was completely true. I had been going through the motions, surviving because it was expected, hoping because there had been hope to have, but all the while there had been a deadened hole inside of me. There had been an emptiness that kept me teetering on the edge of a bleak precipice. The hole, the emptiness would always be there, I knew that, but I wanted to live, I wanted to *survive*. I wasn't ready for this to be the end and I was frightened of what the hospital held for us. I should be elated we had reached our goal, but I was almost certain that we wouldn't be leaving that building.

Tears burned my eyes and throat; I kept my head bowed as I watched every step I took. I didn't realize we had made it to the bottom of the hill until the ground leveled out before me. Lloyd knelt to rest one hand upon the ground as he stopped to survey the buildings.

"Does anyone know the layout?"

"I've been here once before, when my mom's friend had a baby. If you want to know where the maternity ward is, I'm your guy."

Lloyd scowled at Bret before turning his attention back to the hospital. "Bishop said that the pathology and laboratory departments were where we would find the things we need. They're probably located in the main building's basement. Hopefully," I added.

"Now that is useful info," Lloyd muttered.

We hurried through the deepening shadows of the day as we stayed low and scurried across the ground. Lloyd made it to the doors first. He didn't hesitate, as I would have, before plunging into the murky interior. Bret followed behind swiftly but Jenna balked slightly before disappearing inside after them.

I took a deep breath and plunged forward, half afraid that something was going to snag me as soon as I stepped inside. Instead, I entered a world of utter chaos and destruction. I skid to a halt behind Bret; the squeak of my sneakers on the linoleum floor seemed as loud as a gunshot in the eerily silent hall. I winced involuntarily and braced myself for something to come rushing at us out of the shadows. Fortunately nothing moved, nothing stirred; there was nothing left to make a sound.

"What the hell?" Jenna whispered.

There didn't appear to be one inch of the hall that wasn't littered with some type of debris. Papers, medical tools, clothes, blankets, mattresses, pillows, and so many other numerous things covered the floor that it was difficult to differentiate one thing from another. It looked as if a bomb had gone off, but I knew it was something far worse and far more sinister.

"My God." Jenna's hand flew to her mouth as she came to the same sickening realization that I just had.

It wasn't a bomb that had gone off in here, but a feeding frenzy that had left the halls devoid of any life and hope.

"Let's get this over with, quickly." Lloyd's words made sense, but no one moved.

I didn't want to move through the blood that splattered the walls and floor, didn't want to pick my way through the discarded clothing; didn't want to touch the remnants of the dead. I was tempted to close my eyes and block out everything before me, but it was now seared permanently into my mind. The resounding screams that had once filled this hall echoed through my mind. I was shaking as I took a step back. The blood, the horror, the massacre that had occurred here nearly drove me to my knees beneath the crushing weight of despair that was trying to consume me.

Remnants of the suffering remained on the blood streaked walls. The horrendous ordeal of what these people had experienced would forever be absorbed into the sterile white walls of this institution. I could feel the tormented souls of those lost here hovering over my shoulder. They would forever be trapped within the last gruesome moments of their lives. They'd had no chance, no hope of escaping. Whatever had swept through here had been rapid, it had been devastating, and it had relished in ravaging these people.

Almost as bad as the lost souls I felt lingering within the hall was the smell. The copper tang of blood filled the hall; it was potent within my nostrils and on my tongue. There was something rotting somewhere, most likely multiple something's. Jenna was so pale that the blue veins in her eyelids were clearly visible. Her lips were nearly the same color as her face as they trembled and her eyes were filled with unshed tears.

Lloyd had started to move, but his steps were hesitant and wary. Bret followed behind but Jenna and I hung back. We hadn't come through the front door; these rooms all belonged to patients. These doors held endless possibilities and none of them were good. It was like a funhouse but this one was full of horrors straight from Hell.

Slowly we began to follow Bret and Lloyd down the hall. I tried to keep my gaze focused ahead, but every once in awhile it would stray into one of the rooms. So far they all appeared devoid of human remains, but judging by the increasing rancid smell I didn't think it was going to stay that way. The three of them were lucky enough to be able to pull their shirts up over their noses, I wasn't so lucky. I knew I didn't smell good right now, but I definitely smelled better than this place.

"Maybe this was a bad idea," Jenna whispered.

"There's no going back now."

Bret's tone of voice was far harsher than normal, his shoulders were taut and there was a bleakness in his eyes that I despised. Jenna recoiled from his cold attitude and demeanor. I wanted to reach out to her, to soothe her, but I could barely keep hold of the gun in my shaking hand let alone offer comfort to someone else.

A strange buzzing sound reached me at the same time that Lloyd stopped suddenly. I'd never known it was possible but his face turned three shades of green as he gaped into the room on his right. Lloyd's work worn hand trembled as he pulled the door shut. I was extremely grateful for that, I didn't want to see what was in that room as I now understood the source of the buzzing.

Flies.

"Please don't let us find the maternity ward," Jenna whispered.

Bile rose up the back of my throat at the thought but I somehow managed to keep it suppressed. My hands were shaking. My palms were so sweaty that I was beginning to think I wouldn't be able to keep hold of my gun if something *did* attack us. The thought of stumbling across massacred babies was almost my undoing.

For the first time I realized that there were completely defenseless children that hadn't been frozen and that hadn't been killed by the aliens. Some of them had died because there had been no one left to care for them, no one left to feed, bathe, and change them. They had been alone, frightened, and unable to defend themselves against the monsters that had taken our world from us.

A sob lodged in my throat, I blinked back the tears that clogged my eyes. I hadn't thought of those who were entirely defenseless before now. There hadn't been time through the all consuming drive to survive. There hadn't been time through my own grief and loss. Now, I couldn't shake the thought, or the wrath, that came boiling up with it. The aliens would be made to pay, one way or another, I would help find a way to make them *pay* for everything they'd done, and everyone they'd hurt.

There was always hope if we stayed alive, always a chance that we would one day destroy them as surely as they were destroying us. We just couldn't let them succeed first.

Lloyd went in low and fast around a turn in the hall as he moved to the other side of the wall. He nodded to Bret before sweeping further down the hall. We moved more rapidly through the hospital, propelled onward by the hollow emptiness and desolation surrounding us.

The pharmacy was the first thing we came across. The door was open, not because it had been left that way, but because it had been bent in, bowed at the bottom and then ripped upward. The metal frame of the door had been ripped half off and hung at an angle to the floor. Lloyd pocketed his gun, pulled his pack from his back and swung it forward. He held it against his chest as he crawled under the twisted remains.

"Grab as many essentials as you can," he commanded as we followed him into the large room.

Shelves lined the room, dividing it into different sections and blocking Lloyd as he disappeared into the back. Some of the shelves had been knocked over, broken bottles and discarded pills littered the floor. I grit my jaw as pills crunched beneath my feet. I knew that the crunching wasn't overly loud, but it seemed as deafening as gunshots to me in the hushed building. I searched the shelves but they had already been picked over, either by other survivors, or stripped on purpose by the aliens.

Then again, the aliens had brought advanced medical techniques with them upon their arrival. For all I knew we had stopped making any drugs that could have helped us in favor of what the aliens had to offer as an alternative medicine. Fury simmered through me at the sheer ignorance and stupidity we'd shown by swallowing the line of crap they'd fed us.

It had gotten us nothing but heartache and death.

I ignored the white tennis shoe lying on the ground as I moved past the row of antacids. I supposed heartburn sucked, but it wasn't on my list of priorities for necessities. Neither were birth control pills or prescription vitamins.

"Here."

I caught the bottle Lloyd tossed to me and turned it over in my hand to read the label. *Doxycycline.* I nodded as I twisted the top off and dry swallowed one of them. I hoped it was enough to fight off whatever microbes might be multiplying in my body right now due to my injury.

The label said to only take one, but I decided to take another. I was probably going to want some of those antacids afterwards but I didn't care, I wanted whatever germs might be lurking within me to die, quickly.

I was frightened that even now there might be something taking up residence in my body, changing me, or even destroying me. Perhaps eating me from the inside out. I shuddered, and though I knew it wasn't a good idea, I took a third pill before capping the bottle.

I stuffed some extra strength Tylenol and Ibuprofen into my bag but all of the stronger painkillers were gone. I found five boxes of antibiotic cream. I eagerly opened one and braced myself for the sting as I rubbed it over my heated and bubbled flesh. My breath rushed out of me, my teeth grated together, but I was determined to keep dousing my shoulder if it would help kill off any germ or diseased bacteria that creature had left on me. I hoped someone found some burn cream somewhere; it would be good to have something that eased the fierce sting of my tortured skin.

I shoved the rest into my bag and took a deep breath as I zipped it closed. Everything seemed to be going too fast. I felt as if I hadn't had a chance to just stop and think since we'd set out on this mission. But then, what was I going to think about? My father, my mother, Cade, the lost children? Abby and Aiden? It would only pick at old scars and drive me crazy in the process.

It was better not to think, but it was also exhausting. There were so many suppressed emotions roiling around within me that I could barely breathe sometimes. There was so much anguish and loss within me that there were times I wasn't sure I could go on, and right now I was trapped within that feeling.

It hit me out of nowhere, the weight of my heartache threatened to bury me within a dark state of depression. Though I tried to stop it, the sudden longing for Cade swelled up out of nowhere. It rose up like a tsunami, towering above me for a moment before crashing down and burying me. It choked my lungs and throat as surely as ocean water would have drowned me. My hands fisted as I inhaled a shaky breath and tried to reign in the agony trying to consume me.

"Shit," I hissed through clenched teeth.

"Bethany?"

I shrank away from Bret's hand as it gently landed on my shoulder. I could feel the distress that my rejection caused him, but I was so buried beneath my swirling misery that I couldn't acknowledge, or ease, his. I inhaled through my clenched teeth as I gradually reigned in the flood of emotions that had threatened to take me down. It took me a few more minutes, but I was finally able to regain enough control to open my eyes.

"Are you ok?"

"I'm fine." I didn't look at Bret, I simply couldn't right now.

It was all so grueling. *But there was always hope,* I forcefully reminded myself, and we were a big factor in helping to keep that hope alive. I had to keep it together, I could lose it later; I could grieve when we returned to everyone because that was what I needed. I had been struggling so much to keep in control that I hadn't allowed myself to grieve for all of my losses. And I had to grieve if I was ever going to regain some control of myself, if I was ever going to truly begin to move on.

As much as everything inside of me revolted against losing control, I knew that it was starting to happen. I just had to keep it together until this mission was over, and then I would find a secluded spot and cry until I couldn't cry anymore. After that I would cry some more and maybe, just maybe, I wouldn't feel so dead inside.

Though I knew there was no way that I would ever feel fully alive again.

I inhaled sharply and straightened my shoulders. We had to get moving, I wanted out of this place as soon as possible. I slipped my pack onto my back and eased it over my injured shoulder.

"Looks like a bunch of damn vultures came through here," Lloyd muttered.

"Survival of the fittest," I said. They couldn't hide their relief as they focused their attention on me. Apparently the precipice I had been teetering on had been more visible to them than I had realized. "We should go."

I avoided Bret's hand as he reached for me and made my way to the ruined door. Lloyd stopped me before I could duck back under the twisted frame. "Are you going to be ok?" he inquired so quietly that even I could barely hear him.

"I'll be fine."

His eyes were bloodshot, there were shadows under them, but he was far more alert than his bedraggled countenance suggested. "This is not the time to fall apart."

I shot him a withering look. I was angered by his words, but I was even angrier at myself for allowing them to catch even a brief glimpse of my weakness. "I'm fine."

I slipped out of the doorway and kept my gun by my side as I moved. "Slow down," Lloyd ordered from behind me.

I didn't like the idea of slowing down; I wanted to bolt down the halls in search of something, anything other than this unending silence and blood. I slipped around a corner and froze as a strange noise drifted to me. It wasn't the buzzing of flies this time, but a faint ding that rang out every ten seconds or so.

"What is that?" Jenna asked.

"The elevator." Lloyd pushed past me and stayed low as he swept down the hall before poking his head around the corner. He tried to shove me back again, but it was too late I had already seen what was causing the elevator to repeatedly open and close. My hand flew to my mouth as I took a stumbling step back. I could feel the blood draining from my face and for a moment I thought I was going to pass out.

"Just a boy," I breathed trying to shake the image of the mangled body from my mind. He was so twisted and mauled that he was barely recognizable as a human except for his small Nike sneakers, his close cropped flaxen hair, and the bloodied stuffed bear by his side. Lloyd grasped hold of my shoulders as he pushed me back. "He wasn't one of The Frozen Ones," I realized. His body wouldn't still be here if he had been.

"No," Lloyd agreed.

I shuddered in revulsion as I tried not to throw up. Jenna had retreated, her eyes were haunted and she hadn't even seen the broken body of the child. "We have to get out of here."

Though he was paler than normal Lloyd's eyes were remorseless. "Yes." He nudged me toward another hallway. "Find some stairs."

CHAPTER 10

I tucked the bulky microscope under my arm. It was heavier than I would have liked and would soon become tiresome, but I'd finally found my prize and I wasn't going to relinquish it. Not yet anyway. We had come so far and fought so much for this, and a few other supplies. It seemed so insignificant but it could end up being mankind's salvation. Bret and Jenna were busy scooping up vials, Petri dishes, and microscope slides from the counters and cabinets. A fair amount of the food would have to be left behind, but we would find more along the way or go hungry until we found the others.

"This thing's going to be a pain in the ass to carry," Lloyd mumbled as he studied the hematology analyzer from all angles.

"We need it," Bret responded.

I glanced at all of the equipment, there was so much of it, and so few of us. Bishop had explicitly requested the microscope, analyzer, and other supplies but I wanted to take everything. I was certain that if we left even one thing behind, it would turn out to be *the* thing we needed most. There was no way I was ever coming back to this place again.

Lloyd awkwardly lifted the smallest analyzer in the room; he looked completely annoyed by the bulky piece of equipment as he pushed it into his large pack. He wasn't able to completely zip it closed, but it was still better than having his hands occupied with carrying the thing.

We spent another ten minutes grabbing and packing away as much as we could. I knew we were leaving something behind, but there was only so much we could take, and only so long we could stay within these haunted walls.

We were far more subdued and far less optimistic as we made our way out of the building. We had succeeded in our mission and yet I felt as if I was leaving a piece of myself inside that hospital. Lloyd radioed Darnell and they arranged a meeting place in four days. I thought I should feel more joy over being reunited with my brother and sister, I felt none. In my mind I could still hear the distant ding of the elevator opening and closing on the mangled body of the small boy.

The rancid rotten meat smell of that place clung to me. The blessed sting of a hot shower would be delightful right now, but that was a pipe dream, and one that I didn't expect to have come true anytime soon.

I settled against a small maple and drew my knees up to my chest as I rested my chin on top of them. I had volunteered to take the first watch; I'd spent most of the day unconscious after all.

It wasn't long before Bret's muted snores started to fill the air. I sat for awhile, trying not to think, yet unable to shut my mind off. Unable to sit still anymore I bolted to my feet. Barney opened one eye to watch me before yawning and drifting off to sleep again.

I felt like a caged tiger as I paced through the woods. Even if Bishop could find some miracle cure within my blood, how did we then defeat the aliens? They knew all of our weaknesses and we knew none of theirs. Their creatures could be killed with bullets, but it took a lot to take one of them down, and it was nearly impossible to take down two or three at a time without losing people in the process.

I supposed bombs or dynamite would be better, and one of the soldiers might know how to use them, but how did we get a hold of explosives? Even if we did get them, and they helped with the creatures, the aliens still wouldn't leave their ships. Or at least I didn't think they had left their ships since this whole debacle had started. They probably wouldn't leave them either until they felt it was safer for them to come down here. They were human in appearance, though they didn't have human compassion or even an ounce of sympathy, but it would be easier for our bullets to take them down and they were aware of that fact.

No, they wouldn't come down here. They would leave their dirty work to those things stalking and destroying us. Was this it then? Was this all that we would ever have until they discovered us? Until they killed us?

The savaged body of the little boy flashed through my mind. What they had done to him had been brutal, sadistic, and spiteful. They had made him pay for surviving The Freezing. They would make us pay even worse for fighting them. What had they done to Cade?

I fought against the depression and hopelessness threatening to bury me within their callous grasps. I couldn't think about what they had done to him, couldn't think about how awful his last moments must have been. I couldn't think about the possibility that he could still be alive, that they could still be using him as their play toy, they could still be...

I shuddered as I abruptly shut that train of thought off. It was a train that's only stop was insanity station.

"Bethany?" I turned a little toward Bret but I was unable to fully meet his gaze. I was afraid he would see too much of my thoughts if I looked at him. "Are you ok?"

I managed a small nod. He rested his hand on my shoulder as he came to stand beside me. I thought I should move away from his touch, but it felt good to have the comfort of another human being. There weren't many of us left. "I miss Abby and Aiden."

Bret's his hand tensed on my shoulder. "And him."

I closed my eyes and took a breath before turning back to him. Bret had always possessed a youthful air of optimism and innocence that was both endearing and captivating. In this moment he appeared far older than I had ever expected to see him. He wasn't the young boy who had been my boyfriend, or even the young man that had been my friend.

It wasn't just the dark circles under his eyes, but also the bleakness that now haunted them. I wondered what I must look like to him now, how haunted, beaten, and aged I must seem too.

"Yes, and him," I breathed, the constriction in my chest made it difficult to get the words out.

I winced, hating myself as something shifted and changed within Bret's eyes. Grief bloomed in his gaze, but there was something more, something else coming to life within his caring gaze. "I thought it was just a whim, just the heat of the moment and the fear of death that brought the two of you together. But it *was* more, wasn't it?"

I was finding it increasingly difficult to breathe. "Yes. I *never* meant to hurt you Bret. I love you."

"I know you do, but not in the same way that you love him."

I couldn't respond to that; there wasn't anything I could say to make any of this better. We had all been wounded, I didn't want the pain to continue, but it had only been a matter of time before we had this conversation, and it was past time to get it over with. "No."

"You're not in love with me."

"No, I'm not."

"You never were."

"I'm sorry Bret. You deserve better, you deserve someone who can give you what you need, and I can't. That part of me is gone."

He was silent for a few minutes. "It doesn't have to be."

He pushed back a strand of my hair as it fell across my face. His fingers lingered on my cheek. "Bret..."

"I'm not saying for me Bethany," he assured me quickly. "I get that it's not going to be us, I understand that now. Maybe one day you'll be able to find someone else, someone that won't be able to take his place, but that you might love again."

I couldn't stop the single tear that slipped free. His words were reasonable, they made sense, but I knew they were wrong. I could live another fifty years (the way things were going that was unlikely), but in those fifty years there would never be someone who would be able to take Cade's place. I didn't have a heart left to give to someone else.

"I am sorry Bret. I *do* love you."

He smiled wanly and stroked my cheek one last time before letting me go. "I know you do, and though I'm working on changing my view of our relationship, I will always love you too."

I smiled as I wrapped my arms around his waist and hugged him. He held me close before releasing me. He ran a hand through his ruffled blond locks and tried to hide his chagrin at my words. "Jenna is actually a really pleasant person. She's different than she used to be," I told him.

Bret shrugged; his eyes were unfocused as he stared into the distance. "She's handling all this better than I'd thought she would," he muttered. He was still obtuse to Jenna's feelings for him but I thought with some nudging, and a little time, he would eventually come around. "We should wake the others; the sun's going to be up soon."

I watched him as he walked back toward Jenna and Lloyd. I felt a little better as some of my burden was lifted from my shoulders. There were many others to carry still, but I was certain that we could all get through them together.

***

"Bethany!" Abby squealed as she raced toward me. She flung herself against me with enough force to knock me back a good foot. Her small arms encircled my waist as she hung onto me with the tenacity of a burr.

I inhaled a raggedy breath. Before entering the new camp I had slipped Bret's shirt on. It chafed and irritated as it rubbed against my barely healed burn, but I didn't want Abby to see the injury. Unfortunately though, she couldn't see that I was injured and took no care as she shook me. Hissing a breath through my teeth, I managed to hug her back. I reveled in the feel of her small body against mine.

"I'm so glad you're back!" she announced.

"Me too," I assured her as I pat her back awkwardly.

"We were so worried!"

"I know, but we're ok."

"You didn't find any survivors?"

I shook my head as I tried not to think about the things we had found. "No, but Jenna's family is still alive, or at least they were."

"How do you know that?"

I kept my good arm draped around her shoulder as we made our way toward the dilapidated barn the survivors had taken up residence in yesterday. There was a small farmhouse beside it, and that was where Abby was steering me. "I'll explain later," I told her.

She wasn't too upset about my delay in telling her anything. "You'll love this place Bethy, it has hot water."

My heart leapt into my throat. "It does?"

"Yep, it's great!"

It was more than great; it was the best thing I'd heard in days. "Yes it is," I agreed.

Aiden came bursting out the door as we climbed the porch steps. A big smile bloomed across his face as he eagerly embraced me. I tried to twist in his arms but he held me firmly as he lifted me a little off the ground. I'd have to make sure he didn't do it again, but I couldn't tell him that in front of Abby. "You had us worried for awhile there."

I smiled at him as I finally managed to break free of his grasp and remove the bag gingerly from my back. "We brought you some presents."

His grin widened as he took the heavy bag from me. "I like presents."

Aiden had always been the first one up on Christmas morning. Once, when he was younger, our parents had awakened to find him already playing with the toys he'd received. They'd put a bell on his door for every Christmas after that one, even last year when he'd been eighteen and old enough to know better, my mother had made sure to hang the bell.

"I know you do."

I nodded greetings to some of the people I recognized as I followed him into the house. It seemed as if the group had thinned down even more. I was sure I'd hear the reason for why, but I wasn't ready for it now. Now I simply felt like enjoying some time with my family again, and a deliciously *hot* shower.

Molly grinned at me and waved energetically with a ball of dough clutched in her hand and flour streaked across her nose and cheekbones. I waved back as we moved passed the kitchen and down the hall. The house had an old feel to it, but was in exceptional condition with fresh paint and airy rooms that had a homey quality that helped me to relax. I almost felt safe again.

Aiden led us onto a back porch that had been enclosed with giant panels of glass. The sun glinting off the glass lit the dancing field of grass and wildflowers that rolled through the backyard. I took a moment to admire the delicate beauty before me. It may not be the world I'd always known anymore, but its splendor could still rob me of my breath.

My eyes were drawn from the field as Aiden stepped past me into the room. Furniture had been shoved to the side and tables placed about. It seemed that Bishop hadn't expected us to fail in our mission and had prepared for our return. Bishop looked up at us and broke into a bright grin as he shoved his glasses further up his nose. "It's good to see you."

"You too." My eyes were drawn back to the windows though. "Beautiful."

"It is," Bishop agreed but he was already going through the bags that had been placed on one of the tables. "You guys did great. Was it difficult?"

I didn't feel like answering that question and apparently neither did Jenna, Bret, or Lloyd as they all remained unspoken. Bishop wasn't overly concerned about an answer though as he was now pawing through Lloyd's bag. There was so much to discuss, so much to learn and do, but all I really wanted was a hot shower and maybe even a real bed if one was available. There would be plenty of time to talk about everything later.

CHAPTER 11

It was the first time in awhile that I didn't look or smell like a pig that had been rolling around in the muck. My hair had been neatly brushed into a ponytail and was back to its subtle honey hue. My stomach rumbled, but for some reason the thought of food made it turn. I thought that I might be getting sick, but I *felt* perfectly fine. I was still sore and bone weary, but I didn't feel ill. My appetite would come back soon; it was just buried beneath my anxiety. I had tried to take a nap after my shower, but even though the mattress was soft and the pillows inviting, sleep had still eluded me. I sometimes thought I would never sleep normally again.

I was unsure of the person in the mirror staring back at me. The person in front of me appeared older and wiser than her seventeen years. My eyes, once a sparkling vivid blue, were now haunted. They belonged to a woman that had seen far too much, and experienced far more than she should have in her short lifetime.

I had to keep reminding myself that though I barely recognized her, the woman staring back at me was *me*. I hesitatingly touched the corners of my eyes, understanding that it was my fingers touching them, but still oddly disassociated from my reflection. Gone was the young girl of only a month ago. Here was a woman that was tougher, with more pronounced cheekbones and lean muscles honed by lack of food, exercise, and training.

I wanted to weep at the image of me, but there were no tears. Not anymore. I pulled the sleeve of my shirt down and frowned at my marred shoulder. It was healing well, and so far I didn't feel anything crawling beneath my skin trying to take me over. It would eventually be just another scar to match the scars that still marred my hip and thigh from when that thing on the beach had grabbed me. Scars I would always bare to remind me of Cade's death, of his sacrifice for me, and of my hatred for our enemies. *It could have been much worse*, I reminded myself, but it did little to ease the sorrow swarming within me.

So many changes, so much lost and so much that could never be regained.

I rested my hand on the glass and pressed my palm flat against its cool surface. I didn't recognize the person staring back at me; I didn't recognize the person living within my skin. *Harder*, that was the only word I could think of to describe me. Hard. That's what I was now.

I knew that I had to be harder in order to survive, we all did, but this hard? This cold? Abby still exuded innocence, Aiden still managed to smile with ease, Bishop was still excited by the prospect of learning, and even Bret retained some of his eternal optimism. Me, well I had nothing left of the girl I had once been. I retained love for my family and friends, but I wasn't so sure I even liked myself anymore.

How could *anyone* like me anymore?

My shoulders collapsed beneath the weight of my thoughts. I pushed back a lock of my hair as it fell across my eye. I had to get out of here, had to escape if only for an hour or two. Though I knew it was impossible, what I truly wanted was to escape from myself, to flee from the stranger staring back at me. To shed her like a snake sheds its skin.

I pulled my sleeve back up, covering the wound as I thought over the layout of the house. It was funny, the world's population had been drastically reduced, yet I never had a chance to be alone for more than a few minutes at a time anymore. There was little privacy in this world, and only one chance to escape.

I slipped two pistols into my waistband but unfortunately my rifle had been left downstairs. There was no way that I could retrieve it without being seen and stopped. Shoving the window open I peered down at the ground. If I hung out the window it wouldn't be that far of a drop to the overgrown grass below. A month ago I never would have contemplated such an action, I would have most certainly broken my ankles, now I had no thought about such a thing happening.

Grasping the sill with both hands I wiggled out the window and held on for a minute before pushing off of it and dropping to the earth. I rolled upon landing to ease the impact. Rapidly regaining my feet, I quickly scanned the area and bolted for the woods. I took pleasure in the act of running and in the freedom of the moment.

Joy filtered through me as I jumped and darted to avoid obstacles with a grace that I had never possessed until this moment. I didn't stop to think about that, didn't pause to speculate how on earth I hadn't managed to kill myself yet in this heedless dash. I just ran until I couldn't breathe, until my legs hurt so bad I could barely take it, and then I ran some more.

I was *free*.

And I wasn't going to stop, not now. If it had been physically possible I never would have stopped. But I couldn't run forever, something that my body was firmly reminding me of. I fell, tried to climb back to my feet, but the exhaustion of my muscles finally outweighed my intense desire for flight. My fingers dug into the leaves and pine needles beneath me as I fell to my knees. As I lay there, inhaling the musty scent of decaying leaves and wet earth, I found a brief bit of peace. I found comfort in my world, *my* Earth.

I let it wash over me; let it calm me as it settled into my bones, into my cells, and into my very soul. In this moment of utter aloneness and freedom, I finally found the tranquility I'd been so desperately seeking. It didn't heal my broken heart, but it helped to ease the distress of my savaged spirit. It was like putting aloe on a sunburn, it helped to ease the sting, but the burn was still present beneath the cool balm.

I breathed deeply, closing my eyes as my fingers curled into the spongy ground beneath me. It was wondrous this world of different sights and smells and freedom. That was why the aliens had come to take it from us. They understood the miracle of the world that we had forgotten. They wanted what was ours, our planet, our blood; our *lives*. They wanted it, and they were deliberately wresting it from us. There had to be a way to stop them.

But that wasn't what I wanted to think about, not here, not now. Now I simply wanted to lie upon the ground and forget about everything except for the magical world surrounding me.

The forest gradually came back to life around me. Creatures crept out of their holes and dens as they searched for food. I remained unmoving as I inhaled the scents, listened to the sounds, and took solace in the healing ointment that the world had to offer. There were so many scents and sounds. Far more than I had ever noticed before, but then I'd never taken the time to just enjoy the world I'd been blessed with. I took the time to do so now.

I knew I had to return soon, knew I had to go back to everyone, but not right now.

For now I wanted to be alone.

I had placed myself in danger by coming out here by myself. There was safety in numbers, alone I was far more vulnerable, but I couldn't bring myself to care about that right now. I didn't want to die, didn't want to get injured again, that wasn't what being here was about. This was about just being alive, about discovering joy where there had been none. This was about trying to find the girl that had been buried by the woman with the oddly cold eyes and strange face.

Even if I couldn't get her back completely, I sought just a small piece of that girl again. I couldn't have my home back, couldn't have my mom or Cade back, but this, *this* I could have. I was still breathing heavily as I flipped onto my back to stare at the spattering of stars sparkling through the thick canopy of trees.

If something came now I would be vulnerable if I couldn't get to my guns in time, but I didn't care. It didn't hurt so much here, I was able to breathe a little easier. Here, there was a small sliver of serenity that I wasn't ready to relinquish as in the shadows of the forest I finally found a dreamless sleep.

***

"Have you discovered anything?"

Bishop lifted his head from the microscope. His brow was furrowed as he blinked rapidly at me. "I uh, I'm not sure."

I frowned at him as I stepped down onto the porch. "What do you mean you're not sure?"

He shook his head and pushed his glasses up his nose as he took a step away from the microscope. "Maybe it's because the blood is old," he muttered.

"I don't understand; you need a fresh sample?"

"Yes, yes that must be it. A fresh sample will solve everything."

"Solve everything?"

I was completely confused by what he was saying, but he didn't seem to notice as he roamed around in search of something. His mutters to himself made my frown deepen and my heartbeat picked up. What was wrong with him? What was wrong with the blood? What was wrong with *me*?

"Bishop?"

He lifted a syringe into the air; the needle at the end glistened in the light and caused me to take a step back. His eyebrows were drawn together as he looked over the needle to me. "It's nothing to worry about Bethy, I'm sure the samples were just contaminated somehow. They have been moved around a lot, and I haven't been able to keep them stored as properly as I would have liked. I'm sure that's the reason for the abnormalities."

I wasn't exactly pleased by his choice of words. "Abnormalities?" I croaked.

"It's nothing a new sample won't clear right up."

"Bishop what the *hell* are you talking about?" I demanded.

His attention had already been diverted back to his machines; he seemed to have simply forgotten the syringe in his hand. A cold chill crept down my spine, the hair on the nape of my neck stood on end. I had been so detached lately, so cold, and unfeeling. What if there was something wrong with me? Was it somehow because of the injury I'd received on the beach, perhaps some strange germ the thing had given me? I'd been dead inside since Cade died and I had blamed my detachment on his loss, but was there something truly *wrong* with me?

My heart pounded rapidly in my chest, my hands were shaking as I shoved them into the pockets of my jeans. I had to fight the urge to turn and flee, to bolt into the woods and bury myself in the solace that they offered. *Not now, not during the day*, I told myself sternly. But tonight I could run and run, and then maybe I could sleep for a little while again. It had been amazing to sleep the sleep of the dead for the past five nights. There were no dreams, no nightmares to plague me within the woods.

Maybe it was the running that did it. Maybe I was just so exhausted by the time I collapsed that it was nearly impossible for me to dream. I didn't think it was that though, I thought it was the simple pleasure of being able to do something freeing, something wild. Something that the girl I'd once been would have been too frightened to do, and the strange woman I'd become would never enjoy. Yet not only did I do it, I also *relished* in it.

In that simple realization I found myself gradually becoming someone new. Becoming someone that wasn't driven by fear as the girl had been, and someone that wasn't driven by anger and hurt as the strange woman had been. The person that was emerging was new, uncertain to me, but I found I was beginning to like her, and I hadn't liked myself in awhile. She was a combination of the girl and the woman. She had some of the same strengths, and some of the same weaknesses, but she had learned and she was wiser. *I* was wiser.

I was developing new ways to handle things, finding new things to enjoy and take pleasure in, and new ways to take care of myself. The ice encasing me was melting; I was beginning to understand that loss wasn't an excuse to hide from people, and love. It wasn't an excuse to withdraw from the world. Grief wasn't something to just be endured, it was something to grow and learn from, and I was finally starting to learn that it was not the end of me.

Those hours in the woods had soothed some of the ragged edges of my frayed soul and had finally allowed me to come back to life, even if only a little bit. But day by day that little bit was beginning to grow into something more recognizable.

But now I could feel the panic tearing at me again, shredding my insides, trying to climb out of me as Bishop placed the syringe between his teeth and hit a few keys on the computer he had set up. There was no internet, the aliens had banned it and dismantled it months before they had unleashed their unholy attack, but Bishop kept all of his notes on his laptop. I watched as he frowned, shook his head, and pulled the syringe from between his lips. He seemed to have completely forgotten that I was even here, or what the syringe was for. I understood this strange quirk about Bishop, understood people who lived mainly within their own worlds. Aiden lived within the walls of science and math; my father had also been a dreamer that had spent many hours locked away writing.

But Bishop was driving me nuts right now, and at this moment I had no patience for it.

"Bishop." He continued to ignore me as his fingers flew over the keyboard. "Larry. Doctor Bishop!" His eyes were large behind his glasses as he finally glanced up at me. I shook my head in annoyance. "What is *wrong* with my blood?"

"Oh yes, yes, your blood. We need a fresh sample Bethany."

I exhaled loudly as I folded my arms over my chest. "I'm on antibiotics, remember?"

"Oh yes, yes." Disappointment flitted over his features and he dropped the syringe down. "We'll wait until you are off the medicine." He'd already informed me of this fact two days ago, but he seemed to have forgotten. "How is your shoulder? Let me take a look."

I sat on the edge of the table as he examined the injury closely. His fingers were gentle as he prodded me, but I couldn't stop myself from wincing as they touched against the tender flesh of the burn. "It's healing exceptionally well considering the amount of damage, and the means taken to close it. It's a good thing you were so close to the hospital as you're showing no signs of infection."

I caught a brief glimpse of a horse head and two front hooves on my shoulder before he tugged my shirt back into place. As the swelling, blistering and redness had gone down the rearing horse burned into my shoulder had become more obvious. *At least it was a horse and not a camel after all*, I thought wryly. I shifted on the table I was sitting on, my hands wrapped around the edge of it as I leaned forward.

"Yes, I was lucky. So what is wrong with the samples?"

He shoved his horn rimmed glasses further up his nose as he glanced back at me. "I told you it's just contaminated, we'll get it all cleared up in a few days."

I knew he was impatient to get fresh samples from me, and now so was I. "What are you seeing in the samples you do have?"

"Cell degeneration." My legs stopped swinging back and forth as I gaped at him. "Abnormalities."

"Excuse me?" I squeaked.

He seemed to truly see me for the first time. "It's nothing to be concerned about Bethany. I'd let you know if there was. The degeneration is simply because the samples are old and were improperly stored. They were more than likely contaminated."

"Contaminated?"

"Hmm." He was back at his computer, his head bowed as he read something on the screen. "Due to the lack of room we had to store the alien carcass, and your blood, in the same fridge at the warehouse. There must have been some cross contamination."

I was annoyed by the fact that he seemed to be taking this so nonchalantly when I was a tumultuous mass of raw nerve endings. There had been so many changes going on within me lately, so many things that I didn't understand. Could these abnormalities in the samples be the reason why? Had that thing that grabbed me on the beach somehow *done* something to me?

"What if it's *not* cross contamination!?" I nearly shrieked.

His head shot up at my harsh tone. My terror must have been evident as he forgot about his computer to walk back toward me. "I'm sorry Bethy I'm not explaining myself well."

"No, you're not," I agreed.

"The blood samples I took from you were ruined when the alien was stored with them. Your cells are showing a mutation."

My throat was completely dry, my heart lumbered in my chest. That cold chill crept down my spine again and left a layer of sweat in its wake. Bishop's eyes grew distant as his eyebrows drew together. I hated the fact that he seemed completely baffled by whatever he had discovered in my cells.

"A mutation that resembles the cells of that thing we killed?" I croaked.

"No, not like that, it's different." I was trying not to shake, trying to remain calm, but it was taking every ounce of strength I had to do so. "The alien cells must have mixed with your blood while they were in the fridge, that's the only thing that makes sense."

"Do you believe there's something different about me? That my cells are different?" My voice was barely more than a whisper.

"No Bethany, I don't believe that. Your cells couldn't be anywhere near as different as what I'm seeing. There are still many human characteristics visible, but the differences are too vast, and too startling. Your DNA would have been changed at a genetic level; it would have rendered you something that was neither human, nor that creature. We would have noticed the differences in you if your cells had been changed; it's simply not possible that we wouldn't. That *you* wouldn't."

Of course it wasn't possible; of *course* I was completely human. My mother and father were entirely human; Aiden and Abby were entirely human. Yet I couldn't shake the feeling that there was something off; that I wasn't entirely like him, like *them*. Not anymore anyway. I *had* noticed differences, not many, and I could explain all of them away by our strange new world and new existence.

Well, my new eating habits were a bit strange, but even that could be explained away. I had eaten very little red meat before all of this had started, but lately it seemed to be all I craved. I also preferred it rare, or at least a lot rarer than I'd ever liked it before. I shuddered at the thought of the still bleeding meat, but even as disgust rolled through me, my stomach rumbled in hungry expectation.

However, even that could be explained away by anemia or some other vitamin that my body was lacking due to my increased exercise and lack of a consistent, and well balanced, diet.

My better night vision was due to my increased night activity. Even my hearing seemed better, but I attributed that to the fact that I used the sense a lot more now in order to survive. I was more graceful and faster because I had to be. Circumstances had honed me into more of an athlete and I had been trained to fight and move more quietly through the world. I was more aware of my body now than I'd ever been, and that was the only reason I noticed all of these differences in me.

Even as I thought it though, I had the niggling doubt that I was wrong, that I was lying to myself.

"You haven't noticed anything have you Bethany?" His gaze was keen and more astute than I liked.

I swallowed heavily as I shook my head. "No, nothing," I lied though he didn't know that. "Aiden and Abby's blood is normal?" I managed to choke out as I wondered if perhaps their blood was abnormal too.

"Their blood's normal, I checked it to see if maybe there was some strange genetic flaw in the three of you."

"Am I…" I broke off as I nearly choked on the words. "Am I somehow one of those things? When that thing grabbed me on the beach, did it somehow do something to me that changed me?"

Bishop chuckled as he shook his head. "That thing didn't change you, I assure you. There are others here, Darnell and Lisa Blake have been grabbed by those things and lived to tell the tale. Their blood is still perfectly fine, I made sure of it. It was just cross contamination Bethany."

Though he said the words, I could tell that even he wasn't completely convinced of them. He was troubled, that much was clear, but he was trying to hide it from me. We both knew that my blood had never been like anyone else's here to begin with. My stomach rolled over, I was going to be sick, but not in front of Bishop. I didn't want him to know that there were a few doubts of my own rolling rapidly through my head.

I *had* to be like everyone else. Abby and Aiden were, my parents had been, and just what else *could* I be? If that thing hadn't changed the others, why would it change me? I had been hit twice by one of them, but these blood samples were drawn before that thing had gotten a hold of me in Plymouth. There was no answer to any of my questions; Bishop had to be right about it just being cross contamination.

Then why was I suddenly terrified of giving Bishop a fresh sample of my blood?

I raptly studied Bishop, but couldn't come up with any reason not to give him blood when I'd given it so freely before. The antibiotics were keeping me safe, for now, but what would happen when I came off of them? What would happen if he took a fresh sample and discovered that there was something wrong with me?

Bishop tenderly touched my arm, but I found no comfort in his kind gesture. My hand trembled as I briefly squeezed his hand. I couldn't shake the unease that twisted within my belly like a poisonous snake as I watched him walk away. I tried to convince myself that Bishop was right, that cross contamination was the culprit, but it wouldn't sink in. There was something else, something savage clamoring inside of me, something begging to be heard.

I couldn't help but feel that it was the voice of truth.

CHAPTER 12

I ran that night. I ran like I had never run before. I ran like all of the dead had risen from their graves and were pursuing me through the trees. Ran like I could escape the blood thumping through my veins, if it even wasn't *my* blood anymore. I was certain that a strange alien entity was pulsing through my veins now. My blood was something that I couldn't escape from, it was the very life of me and it felt like my enemy right now.

It was inside of me, pushing me faster, driving me onward as it tore at my insides.

I wanted to shout my horror to the world. Wanted to fall to my knees and scream until I couldn't scream anymore. But that would only bring *them*, and if they came, they would kill me. If they came they would split me open, like they had that boy in the hospital, and poke around inside me to see if they could find what made me different too. I wondered if they would finally be able to discover what Bishop was so desperately seeking.

I stumbled and fell but scrambled back to my feet. My knees ached from the impact, but I kept going. My labored breathing was harsh in my ears, I fell again as exhaustion buckled my legs. I attempted to get back on my feet, but slipped in the loose leaves and plummeted back to the ground. I lay there, wheezing for breath and trying not to cry as my fingers dug into the earth.

What was *wrong* with me?

I didn't mean what was wrong with my blood, but simply what was wrong with *me*. Why couldn't I be like the others? Why couldn't I put on a smile and at least attempt to fake happiness? Was it because there really was something wrong with me, wrong with my blood?

I shoved myself off the ground, refusing to lay there and be depressed, refusing to be weak and broken anymore.

The woods were my place, this was *my* time. I wouldn't allow it to be ruined, not now, not *ever*. There was nothing wrong with me. I had to believe that. There was nothing wrong with me other than a broken heart, savaged spirit, and a body depleted of the essentials it required.

I saw better at night because now I was a part of the night in a way that I never had been before. I could hear better now because I had learned to listen better, because it was a sense I needed for survival and I had honed it. I was stronger and faster because I had been training, I had lost weight and gained muscle, and I had been *fighting*. I wasn't going to stop fighting now, even if the enemy was within me. I would beat it; I would pick myself up and carry on because that was what had to be done, because that was the way all of our lives were now.

My lungs burned, my legs were weak from the run, but it felt good. I felt *alive*. I wasn't trying to run from myself, wasn't trying to escape something inside of me, I was simply seeking some kind of freedom in a world that was very constricted now.

I ached for Cade and longed for him desperately. He wouldn't have the answers to the questions that plagued me, but his presence had always been comforting and reassuring. He'd always been so strong, so calm, cool, and collected even when I was breaking down and falling apart. He'd made me stronger and I knew he could ease the doubts and crawling horror building within my belly.

I closed my eyes and lay down. The ground was blissfully cool against my heated flesh as my body eased onto the spongy ground. The smell of earth rose up around me, reminding of the delicious aroma of earth and spices that Cade had exuded. I could almost feel him; almost touch the carved muscles beneath his smooth, supple skin. Those eyes, so black and beautiful they had seemed as endless as the night sky, seemed to stretch into an infinity of love and understanding.

A tear slid down my cheek, I didn't try to stop it. Aching loneliness spread through my chest, but I didn't try to push it away or rebury it. It felt good to grieve and for the first time it actually felt good to think of Cade again. It brought agony with it, but it also brought a rush of joy so bittersweet that I almost laughed aloud with it.

My arms shook as I pushed myself up. I sat on the ground, my legs crossed before me as I finally caught my breath. I opened my ears to take in the sounds around me, but I was horrified to realize that the forest was more hushed than normal. Rising to my knees, I caught the faint sounds of animals moving about, but they were far more remote and hesitant. The breath froze in my lungs as I surveyed the woods, looking for the threat that must be lurking within the dense cluster of trees.

I shoved myself up; my legs still trembled from the exertion of my run, but they were strong enough to get me out of here if they had to. My hands went to my waistband, instinctively pulling out one of the guns tucked there. Something seemed to shimmer on my right and I turned in that direction as I leveled my pistol on the tree line. I waited breathlessly, counting the seconds but I didn't see anything else.

My eyes narrowed as I turned in a circle in search of something lurking in the darkness. My senses hummed as I strained to hear, or see, anything out of the ordinary. Though both of those senses failed to detect anything, I was certain there was something there, something hunting me, stalking me. I resented the fact that these creatures enjoyed playing with their food before pouncing.

I swallowed heavily; my body was fairly vibrating with tension. I cursed my stupidity for having run this far. No one would even hear my gunshots out here and I had no one to blame but myself, and my desperate need to feel something other than trapped and broken.

My hands clenched on the pistol as the rustle of leaves rattled through the trees. There was no breeze tonight and the animals had gone to ground. My palms began to sweat as I took up a shooters stance. I might be able to outrun one of them, might be able to lose them in the woods, but I was going to know exactly what it was that I was outrunning.

Then it emerged from the trees with an unnatural grace that left me mesmerized at the same time that I felt everything inside of me wilt like a plant without water for a month as my mouth became as arid as the Sahara. Gooseflesh covered my entire body in tiny pimples that made me shudder. If someone had pushed me, I either would have fallen straight over or shattered into a million shards of ice.

My heart, the organ that had been beating so rapidly just seconds before, seemed to have stopped. I felt as if the thing had shriveled to the size of a raisin. I couldn't feel the blood pulsing through my veins anymore; no longer hear the beat of it in my ears. I could no longer make out any noises and I was certain that my eyes had completely failed me because what I was seeing couldn't possibly be real.

The thing kept coming closer, but I couldn't do anything. It was so unfair, so awful. That they could take on human form had become apparent, but that they could take on *this* human form was just heart wrenching. That they even *knew* to take on this form was truly horrifying.

We had always known that they were superior to us in many ways, but now it seemed that they could also read minds, or knew far more about us then we had ever thought possible. That they knew far more about *me*, and *my* mind, than I could have ever imagined possible. If I had been able to move at all I truly would have pissed myself, or curled up into a sniveling ball of snot and tears.

Was it because I had just been thinking of him? Did they somehow have the power to conjure him because I had been thinking about him so vividly? His eyes, his smell, his skin, had I somehow revealed to them the thing they had sent to kill me?

I remained immobile, half mesmerized and half revolted as the image of Cade came closer to me. I could have fallen asleep on the forest floor. I had done it before, and just because I hadn't dreamed of Cade for the past week didn't mean that it couldn't be happening now.

But I knew that it wasn't a dream. In a dream I would have run to him, I would have thrown my arms around him and kissed him senseless until the cruel reality of waking interrupted us. In a dream, I would have been elated.

Here, I was terrified, and on the verge of complete mental collapse. Here, I was going to go insane before that thing finally did me the favor of ending its torture.

Noise screeched back to my brutalized ears as a hitching breath ripped from my chest. My hand began to tremble on the gun, causing it to waver before me. I knew that I should shoot, knew what this thing was going to do to me, but I couldn't move. I felt like a cobra under the snake charmer's spell, entranced into allowing it to strike instead of offering up the defense that Darnell had been instilling in me.

Entranced by its striking similarity to the man I loved.

Its black hair fell across its forehead just as Cade's had. It framed the most handsome features I had ever seen in my life, features I'd given up all hope of ever seeing again. Yearning sprang forth in me as I fought the urge to touch the creature and run my fingers over the high cheekbones and beloved face. I wanted it so badly that I could barely stand as my knees began to wobble. I really wanted to believe that it *was* him and I wondered if it would allow me to touch it, even if only for a brief moment, before it destroyed me.

My paralysis was falling apart as my hands began to shake so badly that I could barely hold the gun anymore. My lower lip was trembling uncontrollably; the sting of tears burned my eyes. It had his mouth, that beautiful full lower lip and stiff upper one. The black shirt he wore hugged the sculpted abs that I knew were under the shirt, or at least they had been with the real Cade. I wasn't sure if this thing would be *that* detailed, but it did have gleaming onyx eyes that seemed to penetrate to the very core of my soul.

Oh God!

My mind was shattering, splintering. Tears spilled freely down my face as a sob tore from me. It continued to come forward with the uncanny grace and confidence that Cade had exhibited. Beautiful, it was just as beautiful as Cade had been, and it was going to kill me.

My hands tensed on the gun. I lifted it up and leveled it at the things chest. It seemed to hesitate for a moment, seemed doubtful, but then relentlessly it kept moving forward at an even brisker pace. I tried to tell it to stop; to go away and leave me alone, but words couldn't escape my constricted throat. I was going to kill Cade.

It wasn't Cade! My mind screamed at me.

A strangled sob escaped me. I couldn't pull the trigger. I simply couldn't bring myself to put a bullet into *that* face, or to harm him in anyway, even if it wasn't him. I knew what that thing was, and what it was going to do to me. I had seen it with Sarah; I had *felt* it in Plymouth. It was going to kill me, it was going to destroy me in the most agonizing way possible, and I couldn't bring myself do anything about it.

Weak, I cursed myself. But then Cade had always been my weakness, and somehow these things knew that. I imagined they were thoroughly enjoying my misery and I couldn't bring myself to care right now. If I put a bullet in Cade, even a Cade that wasn't real, I would be destroyed anyway. No matter how much I had managed to put myself together over the past couple weeks, I would never be able to put myself together again after that.

All the king's horses and all the king's men, I thought hysterically. *Couldn't put Bethany together again.*

My head bowed, my shoulders shook, as the gun jerked in my hand. "No," I moaned.

I hated myself for this weakness. I should be strong, I should fight. I should take this thing down with me. I should destroy it for mocking me, for mocking Cade, and the bond that we had shared. I should put a bullet in its face and destroy it for its derisive cruelty. Instead, I could only weep like a baby as I watched my angel of death stop before me.

I winced and braced myself for the tentacle that would fly out of it, smash into me, and destroy me the way that it had destroyed Sarah. The way that it had torn into my arm, wrenched into my bones and muscles, and seared into my veins. The thing reached out and seized hold of my hand. I was surprised by the warmth that it radiated, or maybe it just felt that way because I was so unbelievably cold right now. I stared at the hand, baffled by the fact that it still *was* a hand and not some tentacle that sought to drain me of my blood, and my life.

"I am *not* one of those things." The voice that it issued was grating and sounded as if it needed some water.

My eyes flew up as the creature descended upon me, they could *speak*? Instead of destroying my face and skull with a deadly tentacle, its mouth claimed hold of mine. I recoiled as its hands seized hold of my face and throat. *Why was this thing doing this to me? Why was it tormenting me so?* I had fought against them, but I was of no real importance in the fight. I was simply a survivor.

Its thumbs rubbed my cheeks as its hands rested against the tender hollow of my throat. *It was going to choke the life from me instead of draining it from me,* I realized dimly and yet I felt no fear. I was too broken for fear right now.

Then its words sank in and I began to realize that those *things* didn't speak, they never had. My body was beginning to react to this thing in a way that it had only ever reacted to Cade. Heat began to spread through my lips, and then my throat and face as it leisurely seeped through my whole body. My chest expanded as air burst into my stricken lungs. My heart pulsed with the flow of blood that had seemed so restricted before. Blood surged through my nerve endings as my body was set ablaze.

Every cell within me came to life; all of them seemed to be screaming forward, rushing to the place where my lips met the thing kissing me. The cells swelled at the touch of this thing, and filled with life as its hot lips moved over mine in a caress that left me aching and trembling for more. The aliens could mimic us, but could they mimic these sensations, these emotions? I hadn't felt this right, this amazing and whole in so long. I hadn't felt this since…

"Cade," I breathed against the mouth possessing mine.

He didn't answer me as his arm wrapped around my waist. He lifted me up before bringing me gently down beneath him. I was stunned, confused and adrift in the emotions and disbelief pulsating through me. It *was* Cade, but it couldn't be. He was dead. I was grieving and finally salvaging the broken bits of me and putting them back together again.

Now he was here and none of it mattered anymore. It was all forgotten as his searing touch burned through every fiber of my being.

His hands were frantic upon my throat and for a moment I thought that he might accidentally kill me in his desire to touch me again. I couldn't bring myself to care though as his thigh slid between my legs and he pressed me more firmly into the ground. His body was hot against mine as his tongue swept in to take possession of my mouth in forceful thrusts that robbed me of my breath. I'd never felt something so unbelievably fantastic. His kiss became more ferocious and greedier as he sought to taste and possess more of me.

I finally reacted to it as I broke free of the chains of shock that had confined me. My fingers curled into his back as I pressed myself closer to him. I couldn't get enough of him as I grasped desperately at him. Electricity sizzled through my body with the force of a lightning bolt; my head spun as I gasped for breath and rode the current of emotions swamping me.

I arched beneath him, clinging to him as his pelvis rocked against mine. His desperate need was overwhelming my senses, as I was entrenched in the relief and love that filled me. There had never been anything as breathtaking as his hands searing over me and grasping eagerly at me.

His hunger and passion was astonishing in its depth. I'd felt his desire for me before but it had never been this extreme, never been this overpowering. It was almost animalistic, almost savage. I thought I should be troubled about the overwhelming intensity but I couldn't, not when he was touching me again, not when I was holding him, not when he was here with me.

Not when he was *alive*.

I didn't care what happened now, didn't care that this was spiraling far beyond my control. Far beyond his, even. That this was spinning into places I'd never been before. Nothing mattered except for *this* moment, and the two of us.

His hand settled in the hollow of my back, he lifted me against his pelvis as he ground against me. Fire shot through me and pleasure like I'd never experienced before sizzled through my body. The motion jarred my shoulder, but I certainly wasn't going to tell him to stop. He could do whatever he wanted just as long as he was still holding me, and was still alive. His mouth broke away from mine, his heated breath brushed against my skin as his lips left a trail of flames over my skin. My chest heaved against his as my fingers dug into his back. He was my only anchor in this tumultuous sea of love and growing lust.

I knew where this was heading and I craved it like a prisoner craves freedom. He was my freedom and the only one that could sate the needs of my body. Needs that I'd never known until he'd walked back into my life months ago, needs that I'd forgotten since he'd been taken from me.

One of the buttons on my shirt popped off as he eagerly tugged it open. I gasped as cool air hit my overheated and over sensitized skin. I expected to feel the press of his lips against my flesh, but they didn't come. I dazedly opened my eyes to take him in. I ached for him to come back to me, but he remained unmoving as he knelt above me.

His hair was tussled from what had just passed between us; his expression harsh as his swollen lips compressed into a flat line. At first I didn't understand what had happened, what was wrong, and then I realized that his eyes were locked upon my shoulder. I winced as I was consumed by the urge to cover the burn marring me and to hide the ugliness from him. He was still perfect, or at least he appeared to be, and I was even more flawed than when he'd last seen me. My body was marred by scars and a brand of a horse, but I couldn't bring myself to release him. Not yet and possibly not ever again.

His eyes came back to me, and though I hadn't thought it was possible, they appeared even darker. They were chips of black ice, brutal and cold, and filled with an anger I'd never thought to see in him and that caused my knees to tremble against his sides.

"They did that to you?" he grated through clenched teeth.

I swallowed heavily. He seized hold of my hand to stop me as I pulled my shirt over the healing blister. "I don't want you to see it!" I cried, feeling an irrational urge to cry as I tried to tug my hand and shirt free of his grasp. He seemed confused by my outburst, but he let go of my hand and allowed me to cover myself back up.

"What happened?" he asked quietly.

"I don't want to…" My voice broke off. I blinked back tears as I gazed at him. "I don't want to talk about bad things right now. Not with you here. Oh God you're *here*. I'd thought you were dead!"

Tears burst free of me as I threw my arms around his neck and pulled him against me. There was no lust between us this time as I clung to him and cried out my misery of the past month. I cried for the blessed joy of our reunion as his hands ran soothingly over me.

"My Bethany, my beautiful Bethany."

I sobbed as I buried my face in his neck and hugged him. I was never going to let him go, never going to release him again. I was whole once more, I was truly alive, and he was here. He was *here*.

"I thought you were dead. I had given up hope of ever finding you again, ever *seeing* you again."

"I know." His hand wrapped around my head as his fingers threaded through my hair.

"I shouldn't have given up, I should have known. Maybe I could have found you sooner…"

"You never could have found me Bethany," he interrupted.

"Where were you? *How* did you get away?"

His lips were warm as they brushed against my temple, supple as they found my cheek. "I don't want to talk about bad things now either." I pulled away to search his charcoal eyes for some sign that he was different, for some sign that they had damaged him in some irreparable way. There was no such sign in his gleaming gaze as he bent to kiss me again. "Tomorrow we can discuss everything."

He wiped the tears from my cheeks; happiness engulfed me as he kissed my nose. "I love you too," I breathed. "I never got to tell you that. You were taken so fast and I thought you had died without ever knowing how I felt. But I love you Cade and I was broken without you. I could barely breathe…"

"Hush, stop, I know. I knew you loved me Bethy, I've always known. I've been so worried about you, so lost without you also. You're not the only one who was broken, not the only one that feared the other was dead. I know what you went through, I went through it myself. But I've found you now and that's all that matters."

"*How* did you find me?"

His smile was unhurried and lazy and so achingly familiar that I couldn't help grinning crazily back at him. "I could find you anywhere love."

It wasn't a real answer, but I didn't care. The only thing I cared about was that he was here! I threw my arms around his neck again and buried myself against him. He placed tender kisses against my face and neck as I stroked and held him.

He pulled me down to the ground, cradling me against his side as his fingers entwined with mine. I couldn't stop touching him, couldn't get over this sudden good fortune as we simply held and whispered to each other late into the night.

CHAPTER 13

I bolted upright the next morning, my heart leapt into my throat as I searched around frantically. It couldn't have been a dream, it simply couldn't have! It had been so real! My lips were still swollen from his kisses; my skin tingled from the lingering effects of his heated touch. I leapt to my feet, tears burning my eyes as I took a frightened step forward.

Oh God, please no, I pleaded silently.

I couldn't take losing Cade again, even if it had only been a dream. I searched the woods desperately as I took a shaky step forward. It had been so *real*. I could still smell him upon me, still feel his lips against mine; still *taste* him! It couldn't have been a dream. It *couldn't* have been.

"Bethany?" I spun around; a strangled cry escaped me as Cade stepped out of the woods. I didn't know where he had gone to, or why, and I didn't care as I raced at him and threw myself into his arms. "Whoa what's wrong? What happened?"

"You weren't here. I thought it was just another dream, I thought it hadn't been real."

He was rigid for a moment but then his arms came around me and he pulled me against him. A sigh escaped him as he pressed his face into my hair and inhaled deeply. "It wasn't a dream. I'm not leaving you ever again Bethany."

"You can't promise that."

He lifted me against him. I instinctively wrapped my legs around his waist as I leaned back to look down at him. "Maybe not," he admitted. "But I *can* promise you that I will do everything possible to make sure that we are *never* separated again."

I tried to be reassured by his words, but I couldn't be. Our world was so precarious right now, so full of peril and death that every day was an uncertainty. My fingers slid through his silky black hair, hair that was a little longer than it had been the last time I'd seen him, as I kissed him. I had meant for it only to be a quick kiss, but our time apart turned it into something more.

His hands grasped hold of my cheeks as he held me firmly against him. A sliver of paper couldn't have separated us as I lost myself to the blissful feel of his mouth against mine. My heart hammered, my thighs clenched against his sides, but I broke away before I lost myself to him completely.

"Cade I've never…" Heat flared over my face and down my neck as the words clogged in my throat.

His eyes rapidly scanned my face. "Never what?"

I couldn't bring myself to look at him as I slid to the ground. His hands remained on my waist as he refused to relinquish me. "Never you know… ah… I've never…"

"Had sex?"

I was fairly certain that even my hair was about to catch on fire. "Yes," I mumbled. "I mean no."

His fingers threaded through my hair as he pulled me a step closer to him. The smile that curved his mouth caused my hackles to rise. "I know."

"What do you mean you *know*?" I demanded thrown off by his words. Was it so obvious then? Was *I* so obvious?

"Bethany…"

"I *was* dating Bret for a year."

He cocked an eyebrow at me, but his amusement didn't abate. "You were," he agreed. "But it wasn't the same."

"You don't know that." I regretted the words as soon as I uttered them, what I felt for Cade was *extremely* different than anything I had ever felt for Bret and I never wanted him to doubt that.

His smile vanished but his eyes were still sparkling. "I do know that." He kissed me tenderly, then again, and quickly once more. "I haven't either, you know."

I pulled away from his mesmerizing kisses to gape at him. "How is that possible? All the girls in school were after you, you could have had anyone you chose…"

"I *do* have her. I told you once Bethany that it was you; that it has always been you, and I meant that. Do you think just anyone could have taken your place, even for a moment?" I opened my mouth to answer, but I had no idea how to respond to that. I was caught up in his words, and the love that brought tears to my eyes. "No, they couldn't have, just as no one could have taken my place with you. You may have been dating Bret, but you were never *with* Bret, not in your heart."

He placed my hands against his chest. Beneath the muscle and bone I could feel the steady beat of his heart. "And you *are* my heart." He brushed his lips over my forehead as his hand encircled the back of my neck. "I was made for you Bethany and you were made for me. *Nothing* could change that."

I was humbled by his words, enveloped by the weight of them. He was right. I had always known where I belonged, always known who I belonged *with*, even when I had been dating someone else. Even when we hadn't really spoken in years, my heart and soul had been his. It always would be.

"Nothing," I agreed wholeheartedly.

The sweet scent of his breath drifted over me as he caressed my cheeks with his thumbs. "Yes," he murmured.

I wanted to lose myself to him, but I knew that I couldn't. Not right now anyway. Soon though, so very soon I could shut out the rest of the world and lose myself to him. Then a thought occurred to me. "But if you knew all this, if this was what you had always wanted, why did you avoid me so much? Why didn't you come to me before I started dating Bret? Why did you leave me all those years ago?"

Something flickered in eyes; there was a small recoiling that he was unable to hide though he quickly buried it. I wanted to grab at him and pull him back to me as I felt his withdrawal. Then he was smiling, a small curve of his mouth that barely tipped the edges of it but melted his eyes.

He shrugged absently. "I didn't approach you because I was afraid you would reject me. I had nothing to offer you, I was an orphan, and most certainly not the golden boy that Bret is. It was obvious to me that your feelings for him were more platonic than his were for you, but I wasn't going to stop you from going down a path that you felt you had to travel.

"I knew you'd eventually realize it was me you were supposed to be with after all," he added with a wink.

His tone was airy and his grin playful, however a depressing knowledge slithered through my mind, one that I couldn't shake. For the first time ever, Cade had just lied to me. I was certain of it even though I had no proof.

I just didn't know why. It had been such an easy question, but one that he avoided answering truthfully. There was something behind his eyes, something withdrawn and secretive, even as he smiled at me.

I was tempted to press him on it and learn why he would lie over something so simple, but I knew he wasn't going to tell me the truth. I also wasn't willing to spoil this brief bit of heaven I'd been granted. It may be cowardice but I tried to convince myself I had imagined it, even though I didn't believe so.

"I would love to stay, but I have to get back. I'm sure Abby and Aiden have started to look for me by now."

The distance in his gaze faded as he brushed my hair over my shoulders. I buried my doubts as I leaned into his touch. I couldn't get over how wonderful it was to have him here again, how whole I felt once more. I'd never thought of myself as boy crazy, had never thought that I would *ever* need someone as much as I needed him.

I had survived without him, but I'd been unable to truly live. Now I could live again, now I could *feel* again. I could smile and laugh without feeling guilty or lost in a world that terrified me without him. A world that, though it still possessed love and awe had been empty and cold without him.

"I wish we didn't have to go either." He curled my hair around his finger.

"They'll be shocked to see you."

I loved his smile. It was so rare, so fleeting, and yet it lit his entire face. It sparkled in his eyes and radiated with his love for me. "No less than you were."

He pulled me closer to him and kissed me with those magnificent lips. All my doubts were pushed aside as his mouth warmed me to the very center of my soul. His eyes glowed with more than just love when he pulled away from me. My toes curled in response to the ravenous gleam in his gaze. I was certain that he could devour me, but I sensed it was more than just my body he coveted.

A jolt of surprise tore through me as I caught sight of something within Cade that I'd never seen before. Something sinister and dangerous that I didn't understand, but I knew it wanted possession of me in ways that I couldn't even begin to fathom.

Had they done something to him in there? Had they changed him somehow? Was that why he had lied to me?

The thought terrified me, but I couldn't shake it as that midnight gaze burned into me. Seeming to realize my sudden trepidation he blinked and then managed a listless smile. The look was gone from his gaze, but I couldn't forget it, and he couldn't hide it completely.

"Cade..."

"Let's get you back Bethany."

"Are you ok?"

"I'm fine." His fingers entwined with mine and he lifted my hand to place a tender kiss against my knuckles. "Lead the way."

I studied him carefully, but there was no evidence of the darkness I'd seen just moments ago. No evidence of anything other than the man that I'd always known and loved. I had to have been imagining things. I'd become so accustomed to the bad, that I couldn't allow myself to simply enjoy the amazement of his return.

I squeezed his hand as I led him back through the forest. Even though my runs were often hectic and panicked with my need for escape, I was somehow always able to make my way back to the farmhouse. Something in my subconscious must have remembered the route because I sure wasn't any good with directions. As we walked, I told him everything that had happened since he'd been gone. Everything we'd gone through, the losses we'd experienced, the places we'd been, and our trip to Plymouth.

In the beginning he asked questions, but the more I told him, the quieter he became. His jaw clenched and I could practically hear his teeth grinding as I told him about the creature that had attacked me. I didn't go into detail about the pain, I didn't think anyone should know about that, *ever*.

It was a few minutes after I had finished speaking that he finally did so. "You trust this Dr. Bishop?"

That wasn't the response I'd expected. I had told my tale and I'd expected that his was going to be forthcoming now. "Well, yes," I said hesitatingly. "He's smart, he saved my life, and he's a good man."

Cade made a noncommittal sound that puzzled me and caused my uneasiness to grow. I didn't know what had been done to him, what he'd endured while imprisoned by the aliens and he didn't seem to plan to enlighten me.

Even if they had somehow managed to change him, I knew that he still loved me, it was obvious. But what had happened to him? Where had he been? How had he escaped? And why wasn't he telling me anything about his ordeal?

I tried to bury my multiple questions and doubts and be patient, but patience was *not* a virtue of mine. Of course they had changed him, of course he was different. We were both different after what we had endured. We were *all* different from what we'd endured.

"Does he have any idea why you are different than the others?"

His question sounded nonchalant but there was a new tension racing through his already tense body. His shoulders were rigid, his eyes relentless and compelling. I felt a piece of myself withdrawing from him as questions about myself reared back to life. I couldn't bring myself to speak of them though and I realized that it wasn't only Cade that was determined to keep things hidden. I wouldn't be able to stand it if he looked at me differently, and if I was honest with myself, I didn't want to think about them right now. Cade's return had given me a reprieve from the abnormalities in my blood, and until this morning I hadn't thought about it again. I wasn't ready to worry about it now either.

"No. Not yet, but hopefully he will be able discover something that will help the others."

"Hopefully."

He had agreed with me, but he didn't sound overly convinced. "What is your blood type?" I asked.

The small smile he gave me didn't reach his eyes. "O negative."

"At least Bishop won't be trying to stab you on a daily basis." I had tried to sound airy but my voice sounded flat even to me.

"He shouldn't be stabbing you, either."

I swallowed heavily as my hand clenched around his. "What happened to you Cade? Where have you been?"

His gaze flitted away from me as a muscle twitched in his cheek. "There are some things that you're better off not knowing Bethany."

"Cade…" The turmoil within his onyx eyes was more than apparent as they finally met mine again. I wanted to push him into telling me where he'd been and what had been done to him, but it was more than apparent that he wasn't going to talk about it. Not right now anyway. "Whatever happened I can handle it Cade. If you decide one day that you can to talk to me, I'll be here for you. I'll *always* be here for you."

"I intend to talk to you every day for the rest of our lives Bethany, just not about this. Not right now anyway."

"Ok. I understand." I said the words, but I was more than a little baffled by his reluctance to tell me any details about his time in captivity.

He stopped walking suddenly. A small breath escaped me as he wrapped his arm around my waist and pulled me against him. "I don't mean to hurt you, that's the last thing in the world that I want to do. Right now though, all I want is you and our future, not the past. I just plan to be here, with you."

His eyes were haunted, but there was a feverish gleam in them that caused my chest to ache. He needed me to understand his desires and accept them. There were things I wasn't willing to discuss with him too, at least not right now anyway. He wasn't asking me to kill someone; he wasn't asking me to abandon my family or go against my beliefs. He was simply asking me not to make him relive his ordeal.

My heart swelled as my eyes began to burn. I wished that I could take whatever it was that had hurt him so badly away, wished that I'd had more faith that he'd survived, maybe I could have rescued him if I had.

"I never should have given up on you. I should have come after you."

He frowned at me as his mouth pursed firmly. It seemed he wanted to say something, but instead he shook his head and pressed a kiss against my forehead. "There was nothing you could have done. If you had come after me we wouldn't be here right now. You would have been captured or killed. None of this is your fault Bethany and it all worked out for the best. This, right here," he placed my hand firmly against his chest as his other hand caressed my cheek. "This is all that we need."

I managed a smile for him but I couldn't shake my guilt. His lips seized hold of my mouth with a growing hunger that caused my bones to quiver as my fingers hooked into his shirt. He was right; this was all that we needed from now on.

"Bethany!" I jumped at the sharp shout that broke into our haze of bliss. "Where the *hell* have you…"

Aiden's voice broke off as Cade straightened above me and tugged the loose upper half of my shirt closed. I stifled a laugh at the action but Cade had no way of knowing that these people had seen a lot more of me than the missing button revealed. Plus, I was secretly pleased by the protective gesture.

Astonishment widened Aiden's eyes, his mouth dropped as he stopped abruptly. "Cade?" he squeaked in a tone that would have made a mouse proud.

"Hey Aiden."

Aiden's mouth dropped even further, probably due more to Cade's nonchalant response than the fact that he was actually standing there. Aiden's eyes flew to me; he blinked rapidly as a strange sound escaped him. He took another step forward, his eyebrows furrowed over the bridge of his nose as he raked Cade from head to toe with disbelief.

"You're alive."

"I am," Cade agreed.

"What? How?" Aiden sputtered. Then he broke into a grin and grabbed hold of Cade's arm and pulled him close in a quick embrace. There had been tension between the two of them the last time they'd seen each other, mainly due to me and the fact that Bret was Aiden's best friend.

However, Aiden never held a grudge and someone pulling a Lazarus was probably enough to make anyone forget the troubles of the past. "This is amazing! It's great to see you!"

"You too."

"We thought you were dead, how are you still alive?"

"Not now Aiden," I interjected. Leave it to my brother to pounce on Cade with questions. He was like a dog with a bone sometimes. I just hoped that this was one bone he was willing to let go of, at least for a little while.

Aiden's gaze slid to me. "Did you know?"

"No, of course not!" I cried.

Aiden frowned at me as he folded his arms over his chest. "Then why did you come out here if you didn't know he was here?"

I took strength in Cade's solid presence as he wrapped his fingers through mine. "I just had to get away for a bit and have some time to myself."

"In the woods? By *yourself!*?" I shifted uncomfortably. "How long have you been doing that for?"

"Aiden…"

"Damn it Bethany!" he snapped. Then his gaze slid to Cade. "I hope that is over now."

"I like the woods, they're peaceful and I found solace in them."

"And now you won't have to."

I glared at Aiden, he may be right, but that didn't mean I didn't feel like beating him right now. Cade knew that I loved him, that I had been lost without him, but I didn't want him to think I was moping around for the past month, even if I had been. I wanted him to think that I was strong, that I had been surviving and not trying to kill myself. I didn't want him to think that I'd quit and given up, when I hadn't.

"I like being *alone* in the woods," I grated out.

"Not anymore." I shot Cade a disapproving look as he interjected. "I'll be coming with you now."

I wanted to argue with him for taking Aiden's side and tell him that I was fine on my own, but I simply didn't have it in me. All I could do was smile up at him as the memory of last night flitted across my mind. In all honesty I didn't really care if I went into the woods on my own again, or not. I'd much prefer to have him by my side there.

***

Cade stood in the doorway, his arms folded over his chest, his eyes hooded as he surveyed the room. Though his posture was casual there was an underlying tension humming through his body. Bishop prattled eagerly on about how he hoped that my blood would hold the answer to awakening The Frozen Ones. Cade's displeasure was nearly palpable as his eyes followed Bishop's every move and his upper lip curved every once in awhile.

He'd been back for almost three days now, but much to everyone's displeasure, he refused to talk about what he'd gone through and what he'd seen. For the most part Cade still seemed like the person I'd lost, but there were other times when he was distant and almost harsh. There was a current of hostility within him that only eased when we were alone together, which was far rarer than I liked.

The first night had been spent making our way through the shadows, staying to the woods as we moved toward Boston. We had stopped to stay in an old house sheltered in a cove deep in the woods. Unfortunately, there weren't many rooms and though we slept at each other's sides at night, we were never alone.

Cade's strong jaw clenched, there was a smoldering heat in his gaze that warmed the very marrow of my bones. "I do need a fresh sample though, if you don't mind Bethy.

You're off the antibiotics now."

"Ah sure," I answered absently.

Cade opened his mouth as his eyes darted to Bishop but he closed it again as he stepped even closer to me. It was moments like these, when he looked about ready to punch something that had everyone wary of him. I fought the urge to reach out to him but he would only shut me out further if I showed my concern now. I couldn't shake the thought that though I'd miraculously gotten Cade back, he hadn't really returned.

I was rolling my sleeve up for Bishop when a shout rang out. Leaping from the chair I'd been sitting upon, I pulled the gun from my waistband in one fluid motion. Something flashed through Cade's eyes as a questioning look flitted across his face. I supposed he was amazed I hadn't fallen flat on my face, which would have been a good possibility just a couple of months ago. He moved with me through the house as another shout resonated from outside.

Bret and Aiden were out there somewhere; they had gone out with a group of people to help scavenge for food. Apprehension for them hammered through me and I was sprinting by the time I slammed into the screen door. The weight of my body caused it to fling open but Cade grabbed hold of it before it slammed closed. I flew across the porch and came up short as I took in the crowd gathered in a circle. Darnell and Lloyd stood at the front of the circle, their guns leveled at the young man that stood in the center with his hands raised above his head.

"I come in peace," he quipped, using his raised fingers to flash the Vulcan salute. He was grinning brightly despite the fact that he was teetering on the edge of being shot. I aimed at the man's chest; I was at a good angle to fire on him if I had too, even if he was human. None of us kidded ourselves into believing that the aliens were the only thing we had to be apprehensive about anymore.

The smile slipped from his face as he seemed to finally realize that he was in real danger. His hands rose minutely as he surveyed the crowd. Cade stepped forward to block me as the young man's brown eyes swung in our direction. There was something as sinister and deadly about Cade as a lion stalking its prey as his hands fisted at his sides. We may have had the guns but I was suddenly certain that he was the deadliest one amongst us.

The young man's eyes rested upon Cade before sliding toward me. There was an intense moment when I could almost feel the crackle of tension that filled the air. I would have thought that perhaps I was imagining it, but several heads turned in our direction, in *Cade's* direction. One of them was Bret, who studied Cade with an expression that left me feeling oddly hollow. The two of them hadn't ended things on a good note and the hostility between them was starting to grate on my nerves, but for one instant Bret stared at Cade as if he didn't even know him and it scared me.

"What do you want?" Darnell demanded harshly.

The man was sporting a buzz cut and his hair was black stubble against his skull. His deep olive skin gleamed in the fading luminosity of the day. He seemed affable enough, but there was something about him that Cade did *not* like. "I was looking for some shelter, maybe some food. There is safety in numbers, isn't there?"

"Are you by yourself?"

The man nodded. "I am. Can I lower my hands now?"

"Never told you to raise 'em," Darnell retorted with a wry grin.

The man flashed a devilish smile that caused more than a few of the women in the group to melt as they moved closer to him. He was fresh meat and they were the coyotes on the scent. Apparently pickings were slim in the group; it wasn't something I'd noticed until Cade's return. They'd been circling him like a pack of vultures even though he paid them little attention.

"We have some food," Darnell offered.

"And a place to stay?"

I took a step forward but Cade nudged me back. I opened my mouth to protest but the subtle shake of his head silenced me. "We'll see," Darnell told him. "Lloyd, take this man to Molly and stay with them." Darnell leaned close to Lloyd and said something that caused Lloyd to nod in response. He stepped forward as the man's gaze slid back toward Cade and then focused on me.

"Go inside Bethany," Cade calmly ordered.

I balked against his command. "Cade..."

He grasped hold of my shoulders and turned me toward the door. I felt like a wooden marionette as he slipped his arm around my shoulders and led me forward. He was trying to appear casual but his body was taut, and I caught the backwards glance he threw over his shoulder.

"Do you know him?" I inquired.

"No."

I frowned as the disquieting notion that he was lying to me again suffused me. "You seem upset by his presence."

"I don't want to see anyone get hurt."

"And you think he'll hurt someone?"

Cade shrugged. "We can't trust him until we know him, but it's foolish to give him the chance to do something. Things can go wrong very quickly."

That was a fact that we were both well aware of. The screen door opened, causing us both to turn as Darnell came stomping inside. "We're moving again. Let Bishop know."

"But we just got here." I hadn't seen Jenna standing in the doorway of the downstairs bathroom until she spoke. Her strawberry hair hung in wet curls around her shoulders. Her sky eyes were filled with dismay as she surveyed Darnell.

"Better safe than sorry. There could be other people out there and we don't know if we can trust him."

Jenna opened her mouth but Darnell moved past her before he could elaborate. She turned toward us. "What does that mean?"

I explained it to her as we made our way toward the back, and Bishop. He was going to be disappointed that he wouldn't be able to get a fresh blood sample out of me again. For some strange reason, I was acutely relieved by that fact. Cade disapproved of Bishop using me as a guinea pig, and I wasn't certain I would like the answers that Bishop's new round of tests might reveal.

CHAPTER 14

    I studied the map, barely listening as Darnell outlined the path he planned to take. Some of it was going to be rough terrain, but at least it was mainly woods. We'd been on the move for the past three days, only now settling down again for a rest. We had decided to spend a few days at the hotel we'd discovered nestled at the edge of the woods.

    On the other side of the large, cabin-like building was a sparkling blue lake. Everyone had been ordered to stay away from the lake as only the woods and building were a secure position in which to remain hidden. It was a good thing the weather had become cooler; I didn't think I'd be able to resist the allure of the deep blue water otherwise.

    I glanced at the people gathered around me at the table. Aiden and Lloyd were close together, and Jenna was leaning over Bret's shoulder. It looked like an intimate posture for the two of them, but unfortunately it was simply because it was the only place she'd been able to squeeze in. Bret was still annoyingly obtuse to her, not because of me, but because he'd become focused on becoming even more of a soldier. He spent every free minute he had training with the remaining troops. Bishop was standing beside the two other soldiers, Private Mick Smith and Private Frank Doogal.

    There were a few other people gathered around, but I was acutely aware of the fact that Cade was not present. Neither was Ian Hoyt, the enigmatic man that had roamed into our camp just days ago. Cade was still distrustful of him and he did whatever he could to keep me as far from Ian as possible. I was determined to question him on it, but we barely had a moment alone, never mind enough time to have an in depth conversation. I was hoping that our stay in this hotel would give us a chance for some much needed privacy.

My attention left Darnell and the map as I once more scanned the crowd for Cade. I was concerned about him, but he still wouldn't talk to me about what had happened to him while he'd been gone.

He was like a pot ready to boil as tension simmered beneath his surface. I was becoming increasingly frightened he was going to explode; no matter how firm a hold he tried to keep on himself.

A feathery touch on my elbow pulled me away from my morose thoughts. I blinked Bishop into focus but the others were leaving the room. "We're staying for a few days. I would like to get a sample now, if I could?"

My throat was suddenly dry but I managed a brief nod. I couldn't put Bishop off forever, couldn't hide from what may be hidden within my blood. I wanted to know about Cade's secrets, but I think he suspected I was harboring a few of my own. He didn't question me about it, but I was well aware of the fact that he was watching me more than usual. Even more than those times I'd caught him studying me in the halls at school.

It was all very confusing but neither of us seemed willing to talk about what we were going through, or our doubts. I was even more confused about the changes going on inside of me. Changes that had increased since that thing had attacked me in Plymouth. My craving for meat had intensified, it was a battle to avoid it now, one that left me strained and exhausted by the end of every day. I almost hoped that this fresh sample of blood would provide Bishop with the answers he sought, but I was terrified of what those answers might be.

"Of course," I murmured.

I followed Bishop up the steps of the hotel. He had set up his new research area in the small ballroom tucked in between two larger ballrooms. The three rooms could be combined by opening the partition that separated them. When they were all combined the rooms took up almost three quarters of the first floor of the hotel. I imagined it had been a beautiful spot for weddings and parties.

I sat on the stool that Bishop patted the seat of before turning away to grab his ever present needle. My other, tainted, blood samples had been disposed of. Bishop had seen no reason to keep them since they were ruined, and I was still available for poking. "Do you really think this could work?" Aiden asked.

I started as I spun on the stool and noticed the small crowd gathering around to watch me give blood. I hadn't realized that Darnell, Lloyd, Aiden, and Jenna had followed us into the room. "It's a possibility," Bishop muttered.

"But it could save more lives, if we can get to the remaining frozen people in time?" Darnell pressed.

We didn't speak of it but I knew they were just as aware as I was that we hadn't come across any of the human statues in awhile. Though there had been some destruction and debris left here, there had been no bodies, and very little blood. I tried not to think about the possibility that they were all dead. That it was already too late to save anyone, no matter how much we tried.

"There's no way to know that, but we can hope," Bishop said.

"So they could all be dead already. This could all be for *no*... thing?" My voice squeaked as Bishop stabbed me.

"They're not dead, at least not all of them anyway."

A sharp stab shot through me as I twisted on the stool and jerked the syringe in my arm. I didn't know when he had arrived but Cade was standing in the doorway with his eyes focused upon the needle stuck in my arm. The lean muscles in his forearms flexed as he folded his arms over his chest.

"Who's not dead?" Darnell asked.

"The Frozen Ones."

I could hear a mouse in the walls as everyone held their breath. "What do you mean they're not dead?" Darnell finally asked.

Cade looked away from me as Bishop pulled the vile free and quickly replaced it with another one. I remained unwilling to speak. Those words were the most that Cade had said about anything he'd experienced, or anything he knew. I was concerned that if I spoke he would withdraw and leave us with only those cryptic words.

"They aren't dead. They're trapped in a cryogenic-like state," Cade explained.

"How do we awaken them?" Bishop demanded.

"*We* don't. Those other things do. There's something in them, or they do something that causes the people to awaken again."

My bones quaked, literally rattled, as I vividly recalled the agony those things could inflict. It seemed fitting to say that they could truly 'wake the dead' by causing such a devastating degree of pain. "No matter how much time has passed?" I croaked out.

"I don't know about that," Cade responded flatly.

"How do you know they reawaken?" Darnell asked.

"Bethany and I saw a man come back to life, though at the time we didn't realize why he had come back, and thought that perhaps pain caused it." Abby and Aiden exchanged a guilty glance, and my head bowed beneath the weight of the memory of what had been done to Peter. "Unfortunately, we were wrong. I saw others come back to life too, when those things got a hold of them."

I swallowed heavily, I had never wanted to say the words, but I had to. "It's not the same."

I turned away from Bishop's keen gaze, unable to take the inquisitiveness in his eyes. "What isn't the same Bethy?"

I could feel something inside of me coming forth and then retreating again like a wave on the shore. I wanted to tell them, wanted to share, but it was difficult to find the words. Tears filled my eyes; I blinked them back as I lifted my gaze to Cade. Clouds seemed to shadow his face; there was a rolling turmoil and fury in him that startled me. For a disconcerting moment, darkness seemed to seep through him in waves of black that filled every one of his veins. Then it was gone, and I was left with the thought that I was losing my mind.

"What isn't the same Bethany?" Bishop pushed.

My jaw clenched as I focused on the back wall. "The pain isn't the same." My fingers played nervously with the ragged edges of my shirt. "You can't understand it."

I had almost forgotten that Bishop was drawing my blood until he stuck a cotton ball against me and forced my numb fingers to hold it in place. I was shaking, but it wasn't visible to them. It was an inner shaking that quaked through my blood, my muscles, and deep into my organs.

"So it's worse?"

I couldn't stop the snort of derision that escaped me at Jenna's question. "It's much worse."

"Ok so it's worse than a burn, perhaps if we inflict even more pain than that..."

"No," I interrupted Aiden forcefully. "No." I lurched up awkwardly and stumbled as a wave of dizziness swept through me. Bishop had taken more blood than I'd realized. Cade grasped hold of my arm, but for the first time I didn't want his touch. I didn't want *anyone's* touch. "Don't. I'm fine."

"Bethany..."

I shook his hand off as my mind swarmed with the dizziness that assaulted me with the memories. I inhaled deeply in an attempt to regain control. "No," I said again. "No we will not do anything more to those poor people! We cannot awaken them; it's not possible for *us* to do it."

"A broken bone perhaps," Darnell suggested hesitatingly.

"Maybe, though it would be awful to do, a gunshot," Lloyd muttered.

"It's not possible to duplicate that kind of pain!" My voice was near hysteria and far louder than I'd anticipated, but I didn't want them to think they could do something, or even have them try to do something that they couldn't. "You don't know, you don't understand. So just stop."

"There are other options," Lloyd pressed.

I focused my attention on him. "I'd rather have you cauterize me a hundred times over than ever experience *that* again. I'd rather break every bone in my body than have one of those things enter, and yes I said *enter*, me again. That is not broken bone or burn pain. It is a soul deep wrenching that I can still feel in every fiber of my being. You can't duplicate it Lloyd and to try to do so is cruel and unnecessary torture. Let it go, it can't be done."

Lloyd looked about to argue with me some more, but thankfully he remained silent. I dropped the cotton ball into the trash, more for something to distract me than for any other reason. I could feel them all watching me, but I couldn't look at them.

"They can be awakened though, even if we can't do it." I could feel Cade's eyes boring into me, but I remained focused on a scuff mark on the wood floor. "There are some of Frozen Ones still around, even if we don't see them as often. Sometimes those things just drain them and move on, and sometimes they are gathered and kept for a later time."

I could barely get any air in my lungs as I lifted my eyes to peer at him from under my lashes as he hinted at what he'd seen. A muscle twitched in his cheek as his gaze remained locked on mine. My skin crawled and my insides felt like jelly. I had to fight the urge to press him further as he became silent again.

He reached for me again, but this time he was looking to soothe himself as well as me, and I couldn't refuse him that. I found I could breathe a little easier as my fingers entwined with his.

"Those things left people alive?" Bishop inquired.

"They can drain some of the blood and bring it back."

"Back for who?" Jenna's skin was abnormally pale.

"For the aliens. Those things are like walking storage units. They give their bounty up when they return to the aliens or masters that command them."

"And the alien's, they feed from those things?" Aiden's voice was strained and it sounded as if he was trying not to puke. Cade didn't appear to intend to answer anymore. "What about people like us? The ones still moving?"

"They're there," Cade answered.

Darnell shifted as he folded his hands before him. "There are people still alive?"

Cade's eyes finally left me and slid to Darnell. "I think I'm enough proof that they don't kill everyone, don't you?"

Darnell's eyebrows shot up as his narrow chin jutted out. I wanted to intervene between them but my mouth wouldn't form words. "Where are they?"

Cade shook his head and I could feel his eyes burning into me, even though I didn't meet his gaze. I suddenly understood his reluctance to tell us anything, to tell *me* anything. He didn't want me to get killed or go anywhere near where he'd been held. "I don't know."

Sadness crept through me as I finally met his gaze. "Cade…"

"They're on the Cape, at least some of them anyway, and I think that's why the bridges were destroyed. It's a perfect prison over there for them, an island with no escape. I wouldn't be able to find where I was held again though, they move often." I couldn't shake the feeling that he was lying, that he was keeping something from us. "There is nothing we could do anyway. No way to get at them without greater firepower, more manpower, and a way back across."

"That explains Plymouth. Why the town was so clean, why they hadn't gotten to all of The Frozen Ones yet. They had been too busy setting up the Cape as another holding place for people," Lloyd said in awe.

"We can't just give up," Jenna whispered. "We can't just *leave* them there."

I wanted to agree with her, but there was a knot in my throat that I couldn't swallow. The thought of leaving them behind made me sick, but how could we possibly help them? Not only did it seem as if we weren't going to be able to help the ones that had been captured, but there was nothing we could do to awaken The Frozen Ones.

"My blood isn't the answer," I said thoughtfully. "It *is* those things."

Bishop tapped his chin thoughtfully as he studied me. "It's the answer for something," he insisted. "It could be a vaccine, it could still awaken people. We have no idea the potential your blood may hold."

"Or doesn't hold," Cade interjected. "Just because she has a different blood type than everyone here doesn't mean that she is the *only* one. There could be other survivors like her, and you just haven't run across them yet."

"It's too big of a coincidence. Hopefully these uncontaminated samples will hold some answers."

Cade's nostrils flared, his eyes fixated on Bishop as his hand slid from mine. "Were you held on the Cape?" Lloyd inquired.

"Yes."

My skin crawled. They had turned our home into a place of death and desolation, a place that Cade had managed to escape from twice, but how? I turned back to ask him, but he was already gone.

***

"You can't keep me sheltered. You can't protect me from them. You can't hide the truth from me."

It had taken me a half an hour to find Cade in the workout room of the hotel, beating the crap out of a punching bag. Though I could feel his frustration, I couldn't help but admire the ripple of lean muscle across his chest and abdomen as he rolled his shoulders and stretched his arms. A thin layer of sweat coated his bare skin, his dampened midnight hair curled against his high cheekbones. His eyes smoldered like hot coals as he met my gaze.

I swallowed heavily as I struggled to ignore the heat that pooled through my body and caused my toes to curl. My fingers itched to touch that smooth skin, to feel the heat of him against me. Right now was not the time to jump him though, no matter how much I was tempted to. "There is no way to keep me completely safe," I managed to croak out.

"Maybe not, but I can do my best to try."

"Cade…"

"There are things that you do *not* need to know Bethany. Leave it at that." Walking over to a bench he grabbed a towel that had been tossed there. He wiped his face and arms with the towel before draping it around his shoulders and turning to me. "And there are things that I can do to keep it that way."

I took a deep breath before taking a step into the room. Annoyance battled with love inside of me as I tried to keep hold of my patience. "You were gone for over a month Cade."

A muscle in his cheek jumped as his jaw clenched. "Yes."

"The girl you left on that beach is gone." It was weird saying those words and admitting it to someone other than myself. "I'm not the same, and neither are you. I was weaker then, I was frightened and partially beaten by everything that had happened. When I lost you I had no hope; all I had was revenge and I did whatever I could to try and find a way to exact that revenge. I'm stronger now, I can fight and I'm excellent with a gun. The girl you left behind…"

"I know that she doesn't exist anymore." He dropped the towel on the bench and strode over to me. The heat of his body warmed me and though we weren't touching I could practically feel him pressed against me. I didn't realize, until now, that a part of me had been terrified that he was clinging to the ghost of the person I'd been and that he would stop loving me when he realized the truth. "You *are* stronger and more capable. I loved that girl Bethany, and I love this one, there is nothing that will *ever* change that."

Tears pooled in my eyes. "Then *talk* to me," I whispered fervently. "I can take it."

He took a step closer and I couldn't stop myself from reaching up and resting my hands against his solid chest. Muscles flexed and shifted beneath my fingers as his breath tickled my hair. Though he'd been kept as a prisoner, unlike me, there were no scars marring his chest and abdomen. I hadn't seen the rest of him, but I was fairly certain that he remained unscarred over his legs and waist too. His hands clasped hold of my fingers and pressed them flat against his warm skin. I knew there was something that I had come here to talk to him about, but for the life of me I couldn't recall it anymore.

His fingers threaded through my hair as he bent to kiss me gently. A sigh of relief escaped me as heat seeped through my bones and joy suffused me. His lips remained brushing against mine as he spoke. "You've endured things that I can never take away from you, no matter how much I would like to. I can keep you a little safer now Bethany, I can keep you from even more hurt. Let me do that, please."

I couldn't argue with him, not when his mouth was brushing over my face. He pulled me closer to him as his tongue briefly swirled against my ear. A shiver raced through me as my heart leapt and pounded with renewed velocity. "I just wish you would talk to me, tell me…"

"Later, not now. There is nothing I can tell you that would help."

"Those people," I whispered.

His forehead dropped against mine and his thumbs caressed my cheeks. "We have to keep going forward. There are others that still need help, that we *can* still help. There may come a time when we can help the people on the Cape, but now is not that time. We would only succeed in getting ourselves killed. I can't take the chance of losing you again Bethy, I just can't."

I closed my eyes as I leaned into him. He smelled fantastic, like sweat and earth after a refreshing spring rain. "All we can do is survive and hold onto the dream that one day we'll be able to help them."

"One day we will," I said forcefully. "One day we'll help them. Is there any chance that some of them may escape, like you?"

A smile curved his mouth but it didn't reach his eyes. "There's always hope."

Apprehension trickled through me as his words eerily echoed my dream. They left me with an uneasy feeling that even his kiss couldn't ease.

CHAPTER 15

    Without power, and unwilling to waste the battery in my flashlight, I had fallen asleep with no source of light in the room. The heavy curtains had been drawn over the large window and blocked out whatever moonlight the night might have had to offer. I strained to make something out but I couldn't even see my hand as I held it before me. I could hear the faint tick of the seconds on my watch slipping away.
    I'd been sleeping with a group of people for so long that I'd become accustomed to rustling movements, faint snores, and cries from those having nightmares. I was surprised to find that I didn't like the privacy I'd been craving. I was also used to being ensnared within Cade's strong arms, and feeling the reassuring beat of his heart. However, Cade had volunteered to go on patrol tonight in place of a man who had become ill.
    I tugged on a pair of jeans and a shirt; there was no way that I was going to be able to go back to sleep. It was too dark, I was too alone, and I felt the driving urge to escape. I slipped my feet into my battered sneakers and headed out the door. The only thing within the hall was the flickering lamp at the end of it. My hand trailed across the railing as I crept down the stairs and stepped into the main lobby of the small hotel. I could have heard a pin drop as I made my way to the glass front doors.
    Nothing moved in the night beyond the doors. I was torn between wanting to go out there to find Cade, and wanting to run. It had been a tiring day and I was craving the freedom that the woods gave me. A muted sound caused me to turn away from the door. My hand dropped to the gun at my hip as I strained to hear anything more within the hushed hotel. Though no other sound came, I was certain that I'd heard something coming from the ballrooms.

Bishop was probably in the backroom, absorbed in his microscope and fresh samples.

I made my way back there, eager for some company, and perhaps some newfound insights from the doc. A flashlight was sitting on the counter as I stepped into the room. Its beam, focused on the back wall, was the only source of illumination in the ballroom. There was no way that Bishop could be working on anything when all that was illuminated was that wall.

"Bishop?" I inquired softly.

I watched in confusion as a person shifted within the shadows. Their movements stirred the night around them, but they didn't emerge completely. A chill shivered down my spine and caused the hair on the nape of my neck to stand up. I didn't know who was in that room, but I knew it wasn't Bishop. My hand wrapped around the butt of my gun as I took a step back.

The night seemed to hug their slender body as they came toward me. There was such an easy grace to them, such a natural ability to blend in with the shadows that I was struck by the strange familiarity of them. "Cade?" I whispered.

But even as I said the name, I knew that it wasn't him either. He would have revealed himself the moment that I'd stepped into this room. For the first time true apprehension enveloped me as I realized that whoever was in the room wasn't coming toward me to talk to me. They were stalking me like a wolf stalked a deer. My throat was dry as I eased the gun from my waistband.

"It's you."

The words were a faint hiss that caused my skin to crawl. I took another step back and jumped a little as I bumped into the wall. I hadn't realized that I'd stepped away from the doorway until that moment. It was a foolhardy mistake that may have just cost me my life as I was certain that this was going to turn into a battle for my life.

The man emerged from the shadows and I understood why I had briefly mistaken him for Cade. They had the same slender build and he was even staring at me with the same hunger and tension I'd seen in Cade's eyes more than a few times. However, in this man's eyes that hunger caused a primitive reaction to hotly burst through me as the fight or flight response kicked into hyperdrive.

I remained immobile as I was gripped with the certainty that if I ran he would maul me to death. Somehow I knew that he would, and that he *could*. "Excuse me?" I managed to choke out.

Ian's eyes raked me from head to toe, his lips were a strange shade of red and there appeared to be something on his mouth as he licked them. His gaze smoldered but there was nothing sexual in his eyes. He wanted something from me but he didn't desire me the way that Cade did. I was shaking as I took a step to the right in an attempt to get back to the open doorway.

"It's you." Hearing those strange words again froze me in place. *What was me?* "You're what he's been hiding. You're all over this room. Your smell, your *taste*, it's everywhere." His hand fell onto the hematology analyzer on the table. It was then that I noticed the empty vials littering the table, vials that had once contained *my* blood. "You're all inside of me." My eyes flew back to his as my heart slammed against my ribs. I could barely breathe through the horror consuming me. "And you're *delicious*."

The purred word caused everything inside of me to go limp. He had drunk my blood, and he had *liked* it.

He was going to kill me. He wasn't human. Holy crap he was one of them!

Thoughts raced through my head at a million miles an hour. I couldn't focus on just one of them, but I knew for certain that he wasn't human. The aliens had infiltrated our group for some reason, and he was going to kill me.

"Sooooo good," he continued. "No wonder he's keeping you to himself. He should know that greedy boys always lose their toys. He's been bad though, very very bad as he's inside of you too. He knows better than that. It's forbidden. But he's *in* you, and you *survived* it. Amazing, he's made you even yummier than you would have been otherwise."

Holy hell, not only was he going to kill me, but he was completely freaking *insane* on top of it!

I didn't know what he was talking about. Didn't know what he could possibly mean with his purred words, and strange statements, but I was shaking from their effects. I was filled with the strange notion that I should understand his words, that a part of me *did* understand them even though I refused to accept the growing knowledge twisting through me.

I was terrified that I was going to die, but I wasn't going down without a fight. I whipped the gun up, but before I could fire it he was on top of me. He was so fast that I had barely seen him move. He hit my hand so hard that numbness instantly caused my fingers to involuntarily release their hold upon the weapon. I opened my mouth to scream but his other hand wrapped around my neck and choked off my scream as he crushed the air from my throat.

I grasped hold of his hand as I scuffled against the death grip strangling me. Stars burst before my eyes. My feet kicked against the wall as he lifted me up with inhuman ease. There was something wrong with his eyes, my vision was swimming due to lack of oxygen but I could still tell that there was something wrong with his eyes.

That was when I realized that his entire eyeball, not just his iris, was completely black. I had the crazy thought that the color in his irises had seeped out to completely take over his eyeballs. However, it wasn't just encompassing his eyes as it seemed to be spreading throughout the veins in his face as they stood out starkly against his olive complexion.

I choked and sputtered as ice began to pulse through my veins. Oozing blackness encompassed him. I could almost feel it creeping out and trying to wrap around me. Trying to get inside of me, just like that *thing* had tried to get inside of me. The cool trickle of blood slid down my neck as his suddenly clawed or talon-like fingers pierced me.

Though he wasn't as ugly as those things that hunted us, and drained us dry, he was even more horrifying as he was what those things served. He was what they *fed,* and now he was determined to feed from me.

That blackness was in the air now and it seemed to be coming at me. More blood spilled free as another lengthy talon pierced my skin. Ian licked his lips eagerly to remove the last of my blood from the vials from them. A gurgled scream escaped me; bile swelled up my throat as he bent his mouth to my neck. His tongue was hot against my chilled skin as he licked over me, tasted me. A low purr escaped him; his pleasure was nearly palpable as he continued to savor my blood. He pulled back and I felt like someone was taking a shard of glass and sliding it down my neck as he used a pointed nail to slice open my skin.

"Delicious," he murmured. "Eat you from the inside out."

That blackness seemed to rip into my very soul as it shredded through my flesh, bone, and marrow. My body convulsed and bucked against him. A scream slammed through my skull, spread through my veins, but remained paralyzed within my throat. I felt as if I were being drained of more than just my blood, but also my soul and life essence. It was as bad as when that other thing had gotten a hold of me, only Ian wasn't physically inflicting a wound in order to do it.

"Inside," he breathed.

I couldn't move as I felt my eyes roll back in my head. I was going to faint and if I fainted I was going to die. I found myself almost welcoming it if it meant that I could escape this.

"No no sweetness," he whispered. I could feel the darkness leaving me as he pulled away. The black veins in his face began to fade but his eyes remained burning charcoal colored orbs as he smiled at me. His disgusting tongue moved up my neck to taste more of my blood before moving on to stroke over my cheek. I recoiled in revulsion from the feel of him but I couldn't get far as his hold remained firm upon me. "It's so much more fun when you stay awake. So much more fun when you enjoy every little thing that I am going to do to you. For hours, *days* even. I'll make him pay for being a greedy, treacherous boy. Oh, the joy of it all."

I didn't have time to respond or react before he ripped me away from the wall. He dragged me by my neck as he made his way toward the back of the room. I stumbled, nearly fell, but was held ungraciously up by the nails digging into my skin.

"I'll teach him to try and hide his toys, to not share. You are a rare treat, a survivor, a delicious, scrumptious little *survivor*. It's truly amazing you know."

No, I didn't know; I didn't have a freaking clue as to what he was talking about. In fact, I could barely think due to the lingering haze of pain and confusion that was clamoring through me.

Ian stopped abruptly and jerked me roughly up. Before I knew what he was doing, his hand was at my waistband. My muscles locked into place, my breath stuck in my lungs as his hand dipped inside my jeans. He grinned at me as his fingers briefly dipped lower to brush against the edge of my underwear before sliding around to pull the knife from the back of my jeans. His hand momentarily squeezed my ass before he released me.

"It's not yet time for that sweet one, there will be plenty of time for that after we're away."

My mouth dropped as I was hit with the fact that there was a fate worse than death, and that I was facing it.

Renewed strength filled me; I shoved off of him violently as I tried to pull free of his rigid hold. Agony surged through me as his claws ripped across my throat, and tore into my skin. Blood spilled over me, but he hadn't expected me to react at all so I was able to wrench free of him. His eyes widened and his mouth parted before his jaw clenched and the black lines returned to the forefront once more.

    I tried to catch my balance as I stumbled back but I still slammed off of one of the tables. He leapt forward with a snarl that caused the hair on my arms to stand on end and my blood to run cold. Grabbing hold of the closest thing to me, I lifted the microscope and swung it at him with the full force of my might. Pain radiated through my arms as the jarring impact of microscope versus face shook my muscles and bones.

    His head was knocked to the side, but his forward momentum wasn't impeded as he plowed into me. His arms were like a steel band around my waist as we fell back. My tailbone took most of the impact of the wood floor as my body bounced off of it. A startled cry escaped me, I attempted to scream but the air was knocked form me as he climbed on top of me. Those claws tore through my shirt, his face was a mask of fury and blackness as my skin was exposed. Though he was enraged with me he didn't shred my skin; that would ruin all of his future plans for me.

    I tried to fend him off, tried to deflect his hands as he pushed and pulled and brutally grabbed at me but it was like pitting a mouse against a lion. He seized hold of my hands and slammed them over my head. He pinned my wrists with one of his hands to the ground as I bucked and kicked beneath him. He was so strong, so unbelievably, *inhumanly* strong. It seemed as if he had a million hands, seemed as if he were everywhere at once as he leaned over me and leered at with a vicious sneer to his upper lip.

    He grabbed hold of my cheeks and squeezed harshly. I winced and turned my head as I tried to break the forceful hold. "By the time I'm done with you you're going to be begging for me to kill you."

I had no doubt that he was right as I glared back at him, but he was going to get a fierce battle out of me before then. He grabbed hold of me and hauled me to my feet by my brutalized throat. I tried to pull away from him again, but it was useless. His nails dug into the sensitive skin of my wrist as he jerked me forward and seized hold of my hair. I winced and tried to grab at his hand but he jerked at my hair and slapped my hand away.

He had only dragged me forward ten feet when the low growl pierced the air. I tried to turn, tried to see where the noise had come from but I was forcefully knocked aside. A small cry escaped me as I bounced roughly off of one of the tables and fell to the ground. The flashlight clattered onto the floor and tumbled into obscurity. The beam spun around the room and flashed blindingly over the walls. I didn't know what was going on, could barely make out anything as I blinked rapidly against the flashing brilliance, but the sounds of a brutal assault were loud in the room.

I scurried away on my hands and knees as the table next to me skittered into the blackness. I jerked back, frightened of getting hit by the heavy piece of furniture as it was kicked in my direction. My heart pounded as I searched for the door, but my vision had been compromised by the flashlight and I couldn't make out anything within the room. My skin crawled at the brutal sounds of punching, the grunts and snarls of the fighters and the cracking of furniture and bones as the fighters rolled and tore at each other.

I didn't know who my savior was, or even if they were winning, but I did know that I had to get out of here and find help. I had just regained my feet when I was hit from behind by one of the bodies. I staggered forward, but my leg twisted beneath me and I found myself back on my hands and knees. I strained to get away but one of the fighters was still half on top of my awkwardly twisted foot.

A startled cry escaped me as hands clawed at me in an attempt to gain purchase in my hair and ruined clothes. I rolled out from underneath them as someone reared out of the night to knock them aside.

That was when I spotted the flashlight. I scurried across the floor and grasped for the small, gleaming torch. My hand seized hold of it as an echoing snap resounded through the room and everything went still. I froze, my hand wrapped around the handle as I waited breathlessly in the shadows. I'd never heard that sound before, but I knew instinctively that it had been the sound of a breaking neck.

I didn't know who had won but I was petrified that Ian was going to grab hold of me again. I couldn't move; I was struggling not to even blink.

My heart leapt into my throat as something moved within the room. I couldn't stay like this forever, I had to *know*. I spun suddenly and aimed the beam in the direction of where I'd last heard anything. I'd hoped to use the flashlight to blind whoever was still with me, even if it was my savior. Instead, it revealed a revelation far worse than anything I ever could have imagined and that left me empty inside.

Ian's neck was twisted at an unnatural angle as he lay sprawled upon the floor. Those entirely black eyes were open, but they no longer saw anything. In fact, they would never see again. His mouth was parted and the right side of his face had caved beneath the force of numerous ferocious blows. Blood was sprayed over his face, his clothes, and the ground around him. Though the spectacle of his mutilated body was disturbing, it was nothing compared to the sight of the person sitting over him.

Cade's shoulders were hunched, his head bowed as his chest heaved. Blood splattered his clothes and streaked his hands and arms. I remained as still as stone, breathless, afraid to move even an inch. There was something feral and savage about him right now that frightened me.

Then he turned toward me. A strange mewling sound escaped me as my hand shook on the flashlight. I didn't recognize the eyes gleaming out at me, barely recognized the beloved face I knew so well because that face had been replaced by the monstrous, nearly unrecognizable face before me.

Everything about him was black, from his entirely onyx eyes to the midnight veins standing starkly out in his face.

Primitive. Violent. Deadly. Those words screamed through my mind as I gaped in revulsion at him. *Inhuman.*

Something inside of me broke and shattered into a thousand pieces as bits of my heart and soul disintegrated. He didn't seem to recognize me as his shark-like gaze unhurriedly slid over me from head to toe and then back again. He shuddered as his eyes froze on the ruined remains of my shirt. The blackness had been receding from his face but it swelled back to life and raced through his veins once more as his eyes found my bloody neck.

I was ashamed of the low whimper that escaped me. Ashamed of the complete lack of control I suddenly had over my body and the crushing sense of defeat that descended over me. His gaze finally returned to my face and the black began to leave him again.

My heart felt like a fragile flower that had just been stomped into the ground. I didn't understand any of this; I just knew that there was a strange sense of finality enclosing me. A strange sense that this was the end and that there was nothing left within me.

He rose with a fluent grace that made me want to cry. That grace, haunting beauty, and strange strength I'd seen him exhibit was finally beginning to make sense to me. He hadn't escaped from the aliens, he hadn't broken free; they had *let* him go. This was why he had refused to talk about what he'd experienced, because he hadn't experienced it as a human or a prisoner. He had no answers for us, nothing he could tell us because he'd been with *his* kind the entire time. He had probably *enjoyed* the time he'd been with them. Probably relished in the death and brutality I was certain the captured people endured.

Now that I knew the truth I realized I'd been a fool to think he loved me. He was a monster, monsters were incapable of love.

Thoughts scrambled and screamed through my mind and I could barely make sense of anything as he continued to gaze at me. I wanted to flee screaming into the darkness, but I found myself unable to move. Then he was rising above me like a sinister avenger of death coming to finish what his cohort had started.

The flashlight slipped from my fingers and I lurched awkwardly upward as he came at me. My heart hammered against my ribs, I kept my hands before me as I ran forward blindly. Though I knew it was a slim chance I would escape, I didn't even know where the damn door was anymore, I wasn't going to simply sit there and let him finish what his friend had started.

Not like this, I thought franticly. Not at the hands of Cade. I could *not* be killed by the only person I'd ever loved.

I hadn't made it very far, not nearly as far as I would have liked before his arms encircled my stomach and chest. My back was brought up firmly against his chest as he easily lifted me off of the ground. His hand snaked around and firmly closed over my mouth as I opened it to scream.

"Shh Bethany, I'm not going to hurt you. Stop, please just stop."

Unable to keep them in anymore, tears slipped down my face. I could feel my mind unraveling rapidly as everything within me spun wildly out of control.

"Oh Bethy," he breathed. "Please don't cry." His head fell against mine and he inhaled a shaky breath. He actually seemed genuinely distraught, but I knew he wasn't genuine about anything that he never had been. A sob lodged in my throat as my broken heart continued to beat a disjointed rhythm. "Let me explain love, let me…"

Noise from the hallway cut him off. His muscles locked against me as he pulled me even tighter against his solid chest. Though I couldn't see him, I could feel the blackness against my back as it crept over him again. A primitive growl escaped him as the running footsteps steadily approached.

Cade effortlessly carried me with him as he slipped further into the shadows. I started to fight against him in an attempt to alert the people approaching to the peril that lurked within this room. That had *always* lurked amongst us and that I had foolishly yearned to come back to me so desperately. However, Cade held me with a rigid strength that was impossible to break free from.

He carried me to the back corner of the room. Cade let go with one hand to search for something behind him. I lurched against him, but he grabbed me back and pinned me against him as three people burst into the room. I saw a brief flash of Bret as a lamp flickered on, but Cade pulled me into the other ballroom and away from any hope of salvation.

CHAPTER 16

Cade didn't release me until he had carried me deep into the woods. I felt as if we had traversed miles, and going by the strength and speed that I now knew he possessed, we probably had. The second he set me on my feet, I tried to run but he grabbed hold of my arm and pulled me back with surprising tenderness. I was brought up against his chest, my arms pressed flush against the muscle beneath his blood spattered cotton shirt. His eyes were fierce as he stared at me, but at least they were back to normal now.

I glared back at him defiantly as I strained to break free of his forceful hold. "I am *not* going to hurt you," he growled.

"How do I know that?" I demanded breathlessly. "How can I believe anything that you say, anything that you do!?"

He watched me for a moment longer before he released me suddenly. I stumbled back as he held up his hands and walked away a couple of steps. "Because I have never hurt you before, and I *never* will."

I pulled my ruined shirt over me as I retreated a few more steps. My head spun as I tried to assimilate his actions and words with everything I'd just witnessed. He'd lied to me repeatedly and pretended to be something that he wasn't, *human*. I was filled with the heartbreaking knowledge that I didn't know him at all.

"You've lied to me repeatedly. I have no idea who or *what* you are."

Though the black didn't return to his face, I could sense it lurking just beneath his surface. "You know exactly who I am. I'm the person that's kept you alive. I'm the man you *claimed* to love."

"But you're not a person," I breathed.

Guilt and uncertainty flared through me hotly as he recoiled as if he'd been slapped. I didn't know who he was,

I wasn't entirely certain *what* he was, but he had saved my life many *many* times. No matter how betrayed and deceived I felt, I still loved him, I always would. I didn't want him to feel like I felt right now, but my betrayal and anger caused me to strike out at him.

"No," he agreed. "I'm not."

The blunt admission was like a cold blast of water against my heated skin. I had known it, I had *seen* it, but I hadn't truly believed it until now. "What did they do to you?" I breathed but even as I asked the question I knew that I was wrong. This hadn't been *done* to him.

He stopped in the middle of pacing to scowl at me over his shoulder. There was so much murderous fury still beneath the surface that I found myself taking an instinctive step away from him. I didn't know him, not anymore, but I was strangely certain that he wasn't going to kill me.

"They didn't *do* anything to me. I was *born* this way."

My legs began to shake as he confirmed what I'd already suspected. I thought I was going to fall, thought I was going to melt into a puddle of boneless goop right there on the forest floor. How could I have been so wrong about everything? "How… how is that possible? I've known you…"

My voice trailed off as I leaned heavily against the tree behind me. Cade had been five years old when his family had moved to our town. Cade's father had been a prominent lawyer whose own father had been a congressman. Mr. Marshall had been planning to run for office himself when he was killed in the botched home robbery that had taken both of Cade's parent's lives. Cade's mother had been a sweet woman who'd always smelled of raisin cookies and Play-Doh. She'd been a teacher in our elementary school and had enrolled Cade into the same class as Aiden in kindergarten.

A year behind them, I wasn't yet in school when Aiden brought Cade home for the first time. I could vividly recall him standing there, skinny and disheveled as he'd listlessly played catch with Aiden. I remembered being struck by the odd realization that he seemed to take no joy in the act of playing as other children would, as Aiden and I did. His face had been slack and emotionless, until he'd seen me. I hadn't known it at the time, I was too young I couldn't possibly have understood the importance of it, but the shocked look of one who was just seeing colors for the first time had transformed his face and would forever be in my heart. Forever be a part of me.

Aiden had tried to shoo me away from them. He'd been annoyed at having his little sister interrupting his time with his new friend. Cade had insisted that I stay and play with them though and had taught me how to throw the football the best he could with my small hands and uncoordinated movements.

He'd arrived at our house as Aiden's friend, but there had been an undeniable bond between us from early on. He'd never treated me like Aiden's annoying younger sister. He'd always been patient and kind to me in a way that neither Aiden, nor any of his other friends, ever had been. I hadn't known what love was then, but I did now, and I knew that I had loved him even then.

Cade spent the next three years coming to our home every weekend and at least a few days a week after school. If Aiden went to his house, I would be invited along too, though I wasn't allowed to spend the night when Aiden did.

Cade stopped coming over immediately after his parents were murdered. He had retreated from life and pretty much faded from my life after that. Though he was placed into foster care, we had continued to go to the same school, but where he'd once been a constant presence in my life and a steady friend, he barely spoke to me again. I'd been upset by his abrupt dismissal of me, but I had been a child and eventually I had moved on.

The night of my father's funeral Cade had come back to me, comforted me, and allowed me to cry when I wouldn't cry in front of the others. I'd thought that he would return to me but he had disappeared from my life once again afterward. Though, I'd often caught him watching me in the halls or in class.

I hadn't known how to approach him again or what to say to him. The older he got the more intimidated I became by his good looks, and the aloof air that set him aside from a lot of the other boys in school. Then Bret had entered my life, and though I'd been acutely aware of Cade still watching me, I had tried to move on with a life that hadn't included him in almost ten years.

Then The Freezing had occurred, and he had saved me on the street and stayed by my side until the aliens had taken him from me on the beach. I'd thought they'd killed him or that they were brutally torturing him. Instead they had just taken him back to where he belonged, and it was not here, it was not amongst us. It was not with *me*.

"Lies. All of it, everything. It's all been lies." My voice was choked and hoarse as I tried to get the words out of it. I could barely think straight let alone speak well as my head spun with the implications. "Oh shit." I closed my eyes as waves of anguish nearly drove me to my knees.

"Not all lies," he murmured. "Not everything Bethany. I couldn't fake my love for you."

A single tear slipped free. It left a cool trail down my heated flesh as it ran down my cheek. I didn't know what to believe or what to think right now. I didn't know which way was north and which way was south or what was up and what was down anymore. The world lurched sickeningly, my hands clutched at the tree as I labored to keep from passing out.

Pressing my forehead against the rough bark of the trunk, I clung to it as I inhaled deeply and repeatedly. It took a few minutes but eventually I was able to regain control of my body, I was not so lucky with my mind or heart. I didn't think I would ever regain control of those.

Finally, I was able to lift my head and look at him again. He had retreated to the other side of the clearing. His arms were folded over his chest, his face and posture defensive as he watched me warily. I was astounded, and a little exasperated by the hurt I sensed radiating from him. *He* was angry and hurt? He wasn't the one who had been *lied* to this entire time. He wasn't the one who had just realized that her boyfriend was some kind of monster that fed on blood and whatever else Ian was after when he attacked me.

His eyes were hooded as he surveyed me. "Would you like me to leave?"

"No!" The word popped out of my mouth before I even had time to consider a response.

I was tempted to scream in frustration and stomp around the clearing like a two year old throwing a tantrum. I wanted to tell him *yes*, that of course I wanted him to leave! He had been deceiving me for years; my pride and trust had not only been bruised but pummeled and they were both demanding to be salvaged somehow. The word stuck in my throat though. I could only stand there and stare at him, wounded and confused by everything unfolding around me.

No matter how infuriated and betrayed I felt, no matter how much I didn't understand any of this, the one thing I did know for certain was that I didn't want him to leave. The thought of it was even worse than living with my kicked ego. I couldn't lose him again. But how could I trust him? I knew nothing about him. Or did I?

I watched him as he moved with the lithe grace of a cougar away from the edge of the woods. The shadows playing over his enticing features seemed to blend with him even though there was no sign of what lurked within him. A darkness that had always lurked beneath his surface but had never made an appearance until he'd been trying to save me tonight. He could have killed all of us years ago, but he hadn't. Instead, he had killed for us, he had helped us to escape the Cape, and he had exposed himself to me tonight. He had killed one of his own for *me* tonight.

I was distressed and I was mad, but I owed it to him to listen to him right now.

I swallowed heavily as he continued to stalk around me. He stayed a good distance away from me, but I didn't kid myself into thinking he couldn't grab me in an instant. "I'll tell you anything you would like to know," he said.

I took a deep breath, my hands fisted as I turned in a circle to keep my eye on him. "I would like to know it all."

He stopped walking and turned to face me. Throwing his shoulders back, his chin jutted out as he ran a hand through his disheveled hair. "There are some things you are going to wish you'd never learned."

I was already certain of that. I was also just as certain that I had to hear everything. "I know." His gaze slid over me as my fingers fiddled with my ruined shirt. "But I have to know Cade. No more secrets." He quirked an eyebrow at me and tilted his head to survey me. His subtle nod encouraged me to go on. I didn't know where to start, but I thought the beginning would be best. "You've been here since I was a child, how is it possible that you're one of them when they only arrived a year ago?"

He leaned back on his heels as he folded his arms over his chest. "We've always been here."

I felt like I'd just taken the annual polar plunge into the sea as I sputtered in disbelief. "Excuse me?"

"We have been here throughout history. Monitoring, watching, and keeping track of your developments and technologies. We've even aided in some of your advancements as we needed the human race to survive and thrive as a food supply."

I shuddered and swallowed the lump in my throat. I couldn't shake the image of a human thigh on a plate when he said food supply. "I'm not sure I understand."

He took a deep breath and then plunged on. "Our planet, from what I've heard about it, is much like earth, hence our similar appearances. My people took everything they could from it and drained it of life and nourishment. When they realized what they had done, and that there would be no salvaging it, they began to make trips to find other planets that they could harvest from. There were fifteen in total."

My mouth parted on a gasp. "Fifteen!?"

"There are three left, including this planet that they haven't harvested to the brink of extinction, for now. They've raided the other twelve beyond repair. They left some survivors behind on the other two planets and I'm sure those numbers have increased by now."

My mouth opened but it took me a moment to form another question. "Why would they do that?"

"They destroyed their own planet; do you honestly think they care about others? The survivors were left…"

"For a later time, and another harvest." I felt ill, but the words escaped me before I could stop them.

"At first, it wasn't that way. At first they just went on missions to the fifteen planets to collect supplies…"

"People?"

"Not every planet calls their species people, or humans." That didn't make what he was saying any better. "The supplies were brought back to our planet for everyone. Some were kept alive, for breeding purposes." Yep, I was going to be ill. "Others were slaughtered outright in order to feed the hungry."

"How did we not notice this?" I demanded.

"It was noticed. There have been mass disappearances throughout history. The lost colony of Roanoke in fifteen ninety, the Anjikuni Eskimo village was a disappearance of nearly two thousand in nineteen thirty." I cringed at the thought of so many lost souls trapped, taken, or slaughtered. Yet it was nothing compared to the numbers we had lost now, numbers so high that were almost impossible to comprehend.

"In nineteen thirty-seven, near Nanking, three thousand Chinese soldiers disappeared while fighting the Japanese. The USS Cyclops disappeared in nineteen eighteen with three hundred and six sailors aboard. The Cyclops was considered to be one of the victims of the Bermuda Triangle, a place that supposedly claimed many lives. There was also…"

I held up a hand to ward off any further descriptions of death and horror. "You've been coming here for so *long*."

"We've been coming here for even longer. Those are just the ones that were written about. There was a time when people were far more isolated then they are now. It wasn't troublesome for an entire group to disappear without drawing any attention. Our society is far more advanced than yours and is capable of things that you can't even begin to fathom."

I fought the urge to drive a fist into his face. "Obviously," I retorted.

"Is it any worse than humans that kill for pleasure or greed?" He asked in a voice devoid of emotion. "We were starving."

"You destroyed your *own* planet!"

"So are you."

Righteous fury simmered through me, my hands folded into fists, but I couldn't argue with his words. He was right in some ways, but in others he was completely wrong. "It's not the same and you know it. We were trying to right some of the damage that we caused and we weren't destroying *other* worlds!"

He sighed as he bowed his head a little. "If you'd had the ability to find other worlds what do you think might have happened to them?"

I glared at him, more enraged by his words than I was by the revelation of what he was. "Don't try to defend what your kind has done."

He didn't look away from me as he nodded. "You're right. Humans may be brutal and thoughtless, but you are *nothing* like my kind. We may be similar in appearance but that is where all resemblances end, at least for most of us anyway."

Some of my resentment melted at his admission. "Why did they keep coming back after taking all of those people? If they kept some for breeding…" I choked in revulsion at the implications of that word.

"Because supply no longer met demand." I recoiled from his words and the indifference with which he delivered them. "My people may be technologically superior, but they are greedy and set in their ways. They are unwilling to change; they are unwilling to curb their ferocious appetites for the greater good."

"They'll just continue to ravage planets instead?"

"I didn't say it was a great plan."

"Obviously not," I retorted.

"I know *nothing* of my world Bethany. I have never seen it and I never will. I barely know anything of my people. I was born on a ship and I was delivered here when I was two. My people are nearly emotionless, love isn't known to them. It isn't understood and it isn't exchanged. They take what they want, when they want it, and they don't take no for an answer. No matter what it is that they want whether it is food, drink or sex, they don't deny themselves. *Ever*."

My head fell into my hands and my fingers curled into my hair. Those poor people that had been taken and were now prisoners. For the first time I realized The Frozen Ones might actually have been the lucky ones. "Oh God," I moaned.

"I told you there were things that you wouldn't want to hear." He was right, so unbelievably right, but I didn't tell him to stop either. "They don't think about the consequences of their actions, and they don't care. They're the superior race no matter where they go; they don't have to worry about the outcome. It's what they know and it's who they are."

My head spun with his words and their implications. Everything that he was saying didn't sound like him, but then who was I to judge who he was? "And who are *you*?" I held my breath as I waited for his answer. I'd thought that he loved me but according to everything he'd just said his kind was incapable of love.

His eyes, the window to his soul, were infinite pools as they gleamed hauntingly in the moonlight. I thought I saw love shining within them, but perhaps I was simply trying to convince myself that there was something there, when it was impossible for it to be. Perhaps I was simply trying to convince myself that my deep love for him really was returned as I'd thought, and that I hadn't been a stupid idiot that had simply imagined it all.

"I'm what *you* made me," he whispered.

I was taken aback by his response. I didn't understand it and I most certainly hadn't been expecting it. He stared at me from under hooded eyes that were guarded. He seemed braced for a blow as he awaited my response but I had no words for him though. What did that even *mean*?

"Before I was captured on the beach I hadn't seen my real parents since I was two, and I saw them only briefly while I was gone. Their depth of indifference to me is only matched by my indifference to them." My mouth dropped at the revelation as my head spun. How could he not care about his parents, even if he hadn't seen them in years? The more he revealed about himself, the less and less I felt I knew him. "I was brought to Earth and given to a couple that was desperate for a child. The Marshall's had no idea what I was though when they adopted me."

I finally found enough of my voice to ask a question. "Why would they give you to the Marshall's of all people?"

"During the Marshall's search for a child they came across one of my kind." At the baffled look on my face he elaborated. "There are many of them in various positions of power, or in various occupations throughout the world that can be used to better our species. They've been doing this for years so that when they did return here to harvest on a far larger scale it would be easier for them to take over. They would be able to get the different governments to concede to certain things if those governments had already been infiltrated with members of our species. In some countries they were even the ruling power."

He leaned against a tree and crossed his long legs before him as he continued to speak. "There's a reason your technology has escalated so rapidly over the last thirty years. Though, they were here before then even, manipulating and organizing things so that it would be easier for them to invade."

I pressed my fist against my teeth, tears streaked down my face as he revealed the stunning depths of the alien's deceptions. "Having one of our own pose as an adoption agent was a perfect opportunity for my people to place their children in various homes where the child might one day rise to become someone of power. Even the aliens that were here didn't know when the new harvest was going to occur. It depended on when it would become necessary for a new reaping. Mr. Marshall…"

"Was a wealthy lawyer from a political family," I muttered around my hand.

"With political aspirations of his own. With his background, and family money, he could have risen to President."

A jolt of fear tore through me as my eyes flew back to Cade's. If Mr. Marshall had risen to President, Cade would have been right there with him. He could have been able to learn so many things that would have been detrimental to the human race, and no one would have thought twice about him because he was Mr. Marshall's son. He would have been living in the freaking White House for crying out loud. If the attack on us still didn't come for many years, there was a chance that Cade himself may have one day been elected into our government.

The full depth of the alien's deviousness and cunning was beginning to sink in. They'd been infiltrating us all those years, they'd been living amongst us and gaining control, and we'd never known. We'd been like fish in a barrel, defenseless and unable to escape those trying to spear us. Even if we'd had some kind of warning of their arrival, we never would have been able to stop them. They knew us too well, they were everywhere and there was no way to bring them down.

I really wanted to walk away. I didn't want to hear this anymore, but I found my feet wouldn't move. The human race had never had a chance to begin with; we had even less of one now that our numbers had been decimated. I slumped against the tree as I tried to understand it all but it was just too much and I was terrified by what little I actually did understand.

Suddenly all of those times he'd seemed so tense, distant and exhausted made sense to me. I recalled all of the times he'd disappeared into the woods and come back strangely revitalized. He'd gone hunting, but what exactly had he been hunting, animals or The Frozen Ones? Nausea twisted in my stomach as I realized how little I knew about the man that had touched me so reverently and stolen my heart.

"You were only a child when they gave you away. How did they expect you to control your er… appetites? I mean you do drink blood, don't you? You're the one that said those monsters bring the blood back for them. Ian…" I choked on my words. "Ian drank mine."

For a moment his eyes became completely black again as a sneer curved his upper lip. I took a small step back, a mewl escaped me as the creature lurking just beneath the surface threatened to reappear at the mention of what Ian had done. I saw the murderous fury he had managed to keep hidden from me for years before he took a deep breath and his shoulders relaxed.

"Don't fear me Bethany."

My heart ached for the sorrow I heard in his voice, but how could I not fear him? He was truly terrifying when he was enraged to the point of revealing his inner self. "I tried to keep him from you…" his voice trailed off, his gaze settled on something in the distance. "It's my fault, I should have done more."

"There was nothing you could have done about tonight," I whispered.

His eyes latched onto me and a cold mask slipped over his beautiful features. For the first time he appeared truly alien to me in the glow of the moon. "I could have killed him sooner. I *should* have killed him sooner."

My mouth dropped and a cold chill ran down my spine. He meant it. He would have killed Ian sooner if he'd known that tonight was going to happen. He would have killed him and he wouldn't have blinked an eye. He was more threatening and deadly than I'd ever thought possible. He had killed for me tonight, and I knew with unfailing certainty that he would do so again.

"Cade…"

"Make no mistake Bethany, *you* come first. *Always*. No matter what happens, after tonight, you have to realize that your safety is number one to me. No matter what the cost or who I have to go through to ensure it."

He took a step closer to me as he continued to speak. "The hunger for something other than food doesn't awaken until we reach fifteen, and neither do our other abilities." It took me a moment to realize that he was answering my last question and that he wasn't going to elaborate on his last statement. "By then we are better able to deal with our urges and we can control *all* our appetites if we so chose. We are capable of surviving on meat if necessary, a lot of it, and preferably raw."

It took everything I had not to vomit as his words rang in my head. *Oh God, oh God*! My mind was screaming, hammering, pulsing with adrenaline as I tried to keep my face impassive. Meat. *Raw* meat. All those strange urges, all the differences... My head bowed as I labored to breathe.

"Though under times of great duress and excessive activity meat doesn't always suffice and it becomes necessary to feed on real blood. There are other ways to fulfill the need to feed on a soul as humans aren't the only creatures that possess one," he continued. I was relieved that he hadn't noticed my reaction to his words about the meat. Though, the feeding on a soul thing was a new development and one that was strange enough to draw my attention away from the anxiety growing within me. "Feeding on a soul doesn't have to destroy, or even hurt the person or creature. I just have to take caution not to lose control."

"So then why are they doing this?" I was stunned by the pleading desperation in my voice but what I really longed to ask was why had they done this to *me*? Why had those creatures changed me on some physical level? *What* had they done to me? But I couldn't force the words out, I could barely admit it to myself, let alone admit it to someone else. "Why?"

Compassion shone from his eyes. For the first time since this had all started I saw the Cade I had come to know and love beneath the callous façade he'd been exhibiting. "Bethany..."

"My mother... Please just tell me *why*!?"

His face went blank again as his eyes became black ice once more. "Because they can, because they're hungry, because they don't curb *their* appetites. It's why they had to abandon their own ravished planet to begin with."

A sob escaped me and then a fiery rage surged through me. I straightened away from the tree as I found strength where seconds ago there had been none. "My mother is dead, *billions* of people's lives have been ruined because they can't control their *appetite*!?"

Was I going to become like that too? The question lodged in my throat, I was desperate to ask it but it refused to leave my mouth.

Cade watched me before finally nodding. "Yes."

His flat answer momentarily spiked my fury. Why wasn't he as indignant and incensed by this as I was? "Damn you!" I snarled.

Hurt flickered in his gaze. He took a step toward me before stopping abruptly. "Damn *me*? I didn't *do* this! I kept you *alive*."

I shook my head, but I could feel everything within me crumbling again. My anger deflated like a popped balloon. I felt like a top spinning out of control, as if *everything* was spinning out of control.

"I've kept you alive for a long time now."

My head shot up at his words. "Excuse me?"

He took another step closer to me. "Ever since the moment I saw you Bethany, I *knew*. I'd never had emotions before then, never experienced feelings; my kind doesn't have those things and we're never supposed to, *ever*. I was supposed to be too young to have felt The Calling when we first met."

"The Calling?"

"The Calling is what we call the desire that we develop to touch and taste a soul. For most of us it occurs when we turn fifteen. When it happens, we feel as if the soul is calling to us, beckoning us to feed from it, to savor it, and gain strength from what it has to offer. I wasn't supposed to feel The Calling for another ten years but the second I saw you it hit me."

"Pardon our souls, noisy things should just keep quiet," I muttered bitterly.

"Not helping," he grated. "You have no idea what it is like to deny The Calling, hour after hour, day after day. No idea what it is like to suppress that *need,* especially when I am around *you.*" My sharp retort died on my tongue. I had seen that hunger burning in his eyes, I had felt his desire for something more from me; I just hadn't known exactly what it was for. Hadn't recognized what it was that he really wanted from me, but then how could I have ever known about this? "The Calling of your soul is so strong, and vibrant, and I want you *so* badly. I would give anything for just..."

His eyes closed, his features softened, as for a brief moment he resembled the tender boy I'd known so long ago. Then his hands fisted as he shook his head and focused on me again. The boy had vanished and I was once again faced with this stranger, this *alien,* across from me.

"A taste?" I was unable to stop the thrill that tore through me at the thought. He wanted me with the same urgency that a horse wanted to run, but he'd never touched me in such a way. I had felt it when Ian had tried to take a part of my soul from me, I would have felt it if Cade had ever done *that.*

"Yes." His excitement was clearly evident in that one simple word as he hissed it at me. "But I can't. At least not with you, *never* you."

"Why not me?" It was a strange question to ask. Especially when I should be happy that he wasn't going to drain me dry, instead of feeling oddly deflated and rejected by such a proposition.

"Because I don't think I could stop myself from taking *all* of you into me. I have never done that before, never drained a living creature completely of their essence. But yours, ah yours," his voice made my skin tingle as it became seductive with yearning. "I want every bit of you inside of me. I want to taste you and feel you until I can't take anymore, and then I want to keep on taking until I'm completely sated, but I don't think I'll ever be sated. Not with you."

I stared at him in wide eyed astonishment. I thought I should be more horrified by what he was saying, what he was telling me, but instead I was oddly titillated by it. *Just what did that say about me?* I wondered. Though I wasn't entirely sure I wanted the answer because I was fairly certain it wouldn't be good.

"The *moment* I saw you." His eyes became distant, almost wistful as he began to pace like a caged, wild panther. I watched him in fascination as my eyes followed every movement he made. "I felt the burning hunger of The Calling in my veins. I didn't know what it was, but it was suddenly there, alive and clawing at me with an intensity that no five year old should have to experience. I am thankful everyday that I didn't destroy you *right then* to satisfy my craving for what is inside of you."

My mouth went dry; I hugged myself against the intensity of his words. "Why didn't you?" I asked tremulously.

"Because the minute I saw you standing there in that little blue dress, with those golden pigtails, it awakened something more than just The Calling within me. I'd never known emotions, never known what it was like to care for someone, to possess this overwhelming urge to protect them. I'd never known what it was like to want to be with someone and I wanted to be with you every second of *every* day. You were so beautiful to me, so vivid and shining and I relished in the newfound emotions you brought to me. Your laugh captivated me; it ensnared me and made me want to laugh with you. I couldn't get enough of your smile.

"I never had it in me to love someone before you, not my real parents, not even the Marshall's. Never mind to love someone as much as I loved *you*, and that love only grew with every minute we shared together. Minutes that I cherished as they made me feel... They made me..."

"Human?" I suggested when words seemed to fail him.

"Human," he breathed. "They made me feel human and I wanted more of that feeling. I wanted more of *you*. I didn't know what the emotion of love was and I was too amazed by its sudden burst into me to completely understand it. I simply knew I would spend the rest of my life looking after you, caring for you, and keeping you safe from the menace that I knew lurked outside of this world that you felt so secure in.

"*You* made me this way Bethany, *you* created me. You turned me into something that I was never supposed to be. Your essence called to me so forcefully that it awakened The Calling in me years before it was supposed to be awakened. You made me *feel* when I was never supposed to. As far as I know I'm the only one this has ever happened to, but I'm sure if it has happened to any others they have also kept it a secret. They would do everything in their power to keep the person they loved safe."

His words were so impassioned that I was struck breathless by them as my heart melted. His *love* for me was rare and wondrous, even if it was strange and alien in its origins. He was beautiful, and even though I wasn't, I realized now just how beautiful he'd always thought I was.

"I didn't know," I whispered. I couldn't imagine the fear and uncertainty such a young boy must have experienced when The Calling happened to him. He'd been unprepared, alone, frightened and *hungry*. That such a young child had restrained from taking what he wanted so badly, when that was what his kind apparently did all the time anyway, was astonishing. That he had done it for *me* was astronomical. "I'm sorry you had to go through that alone."

"I was never alone Bethany, not with you there."

A startled sound of distress tore free of me as a wrenching agony twisted through my chest. His words were so poignant and yet so lost that my heart broke for him. All this time he'd been standing in the shadows, watching me and loving me and I'd never known. All this time he'd suffered in silence and all he'd ever had to do was come to me. I never would have denied him.

"I didn't realize, until all of this happened, that I'd always loved you," I told him. "I knew it on some basic, instinctive level that I buried deep within me in order to keep from being hurt by you again. Because you *did* go away, you *did* leave me Cade. You weren't there. After the Marshall's died, you only ever came back to me the night of my father's funeral, but you never came back again."

"You were *never* supposed to know what I was Bethany, what I struggled with. I simply wanted you to see the good in me, to love the good in me. The good that you *gave* to me and that I never would have had without you. I couldn't stand for you to see the evil in me. I had to go away Bethany, and I couldn't come back if I was going to keep you safe."

"Why?" My lower lip began to tremble as emotions ricocheted through me faster than a bullet in a metal room. "Why did you have to go? You never would have hurt me Cade. You controlled The Calling as a boy of five, why couldn't you do the same at seven, ten, or even fifteen?"

"Because they would have killed you too."

That knocked me back a step. "*Who* would have killed me too?"

I could see the need in his gaze for me to understand as he took a step closer to me. "The Marshall's weren't killed during a random home invasion. They were killed because of me."

I shook my head to clear it. "I don't understand."

"We don't feel emotion Bethany. We don't care for anything other than ourselves and our gratification. I was young and stupid and unbelievably bewildered by you. I thought I hid the fact that I was in love with you well, I didn't. My kind noticed something different in me, but they miscalculated where that difference originated. They had assumed that it was the Marshall's who were causing it. After I met you I did grow to like them more, they were nice enough people, but I still felt little for them other than gratitude for providing me with shelter and food. My love for you did not spread to others. I cared for them, but their deaths didn't overly sadden me.

"However, after they were murdered I knew that I had to stay away from you. My kind couldn't realize that they had been wrong, that it was *you* that had changed me. They would have killed you then, and they wouldn't have been as humane about it as they had been to the Marshall's."

I had been trying to remain standing but my legs finally lost the battle. Sliding down the bark of the trunk, I stared at him as I tried to fully process all that he was saying. I was half afraid I might vomit as the full realization of his words sank in. "They died because of *me*?" I croaked out.

Cade was before me far faster than any human ever could have been. A gasp escaped me as he knelt before me and clasped hold of my cheeks but my fear of him was buried beneath the regret radiating from his eyes.

"They died because of *me* Bethany, because I wasn't strong enough to hide my newfound feelings for you. I promised myself that I would stay away from you after that. Promised myself I would keep my distance and keep you safe, no matter what I had to do to make sure of it. No matter how much it killed me to stay away when you were the only thing I thought of. I had to keep you away from them, and the only way I could think of to do that was to stay away from you myself."

My chest was so constricted with love and heartache that I could scarcely breathe. "The night of my dad's funeral…"

"Your anguish was so intense I could feel it all the way across town. No, we aren't empaths," he hurriedly explained at my questioning look. "But I'm bonded to you somehow, I always have been. I'm connected to you in an intense, intimate way that cannot be broken. I couldn't stay away from you that night, couldn't let you go through that alone because your pain was my pain. I yearned every day after that to return to you, but I just couldn't risk it."

I didn't realize I was crying until he wiped the tears from my cheeks and kissed me with a tenderness and reverence that awed me. "Even now." His breath was warm and sweet against my flesh as his lips brushed over mine again. "I should have stayed away from you, but I felt your grief for me even through the distance separating us. I worked hard to keep my own suffering concealed from them in order to convey that I was still one of them, and I did it well. I couldn't leave though. To run from them would have put you in even more danger. They would have hunted me and searched for me relentlessly. I had to stay away, but I couldn't bare your torment, I had to give you hope…"

"My dream!" I blurted.

"Yes, I wanted you to move on…"

"I couldn't. I tried and I accepted the fact that you were gone but I couldn't move on from you Cade. It's not, it's not like that with me, I simply couldn't…"

"Shh love, I know. I understand." He kissed my cheeks as my voice broke off on a wrenching sob that lodged in my chest. "But your life could continue on with some hope in it; that was all I was trying to give you. I only intended to hold you once more, even if it was just in a dream, but when they hurt you…" His words trailed off, his jaw clenched as his eyes simmered with black fire. "If you were killed, I would have known it and to feel your death…"

He inhaled a shuddery breath as the black briefly shifted throughout his entire eye again. I was breathless as I watched him gradually reel it back in. "I couldn't live with that, I would have snapped. I had vowed to keep you safe my entire life and I had failed. I couldn't stay away from you anymore. I convinced my kind that I would be more useful on the ground as I knew more about humans and was more adept at blending in with them. They agreed to let me come back. They don't know where I am, but they believe that I am on their side. If they find me, if they catch us together, what they will do to you…"

"I don't care," I gushed out terrified that he would leave just so such a thing didn't happen.

"I do and you will if they find us. But to leave you unprotected again, I can't." His fingers threaded through my hair as he pushed it smoothly away from my face. His voice was passionate as he held me. "I can help keep you safe Bethany. Those things won't get hold of you again as long as I'm around. Whatever you decide, whatever you want me to do, I'll do it. If you want me to leave…" His hands tightened on me as a small shudder ran through his body. "I will. Anything you want. *Anything.*"

I opened my mouth to tell him that I never wanted him to leave me, that though I felt betrayed and was aching with loss and confusion I loved him just as much as he loved me. We could deal with this. We *would* deal with this together.

He placed his finger over my mouth before I could respond. "But there is one more thing that you have to know before you make your choice. One thing that could make you hate me forever."

"That's not possible," I murmured around his finger. "I don't hate you now."

"You don't know the worst thing I've done."

I swallowed heavily as apprehension trickled through me. I was certain that no matter what he said, it couldn't possibly get any worse than everything that had been revealed tonight. I could take whatever else he'd kept from me, and we would be fine. However the beaten look in his gaze caused doubts to filter through me. What could he possibly have done to make him look like a kicked puppy so badly?

I held my breath, my hands fisted, as I braced myself for whatever it was he was about to say. "It's ok, just tell me."

"No matter what happens, no matter *what* you decide about me, you cannot allow Bishop to take anymore of your blood."

My breath exploded out of me, my hands relaxed as a snort escaped me. I hadn't been expecting that at all. I had expected that he had lied and there were other women, or even other aliens, or something, *anything* other than that. "Why not?" I asked in amusement.

He didn't look at all amused though as his gaze burned into mine. "Because you are not completely human Bethany, not anymore."

I hadn't been expecting *that* either.

CHAPTER 17

I froze, trapped like a deer in the headlights as I searched his face for some sign he was kidding. Some sign that he was going to yell, "Gotcha!" any second. Some sign that this was some sick, twisted joke that only an alien, with their quirky sense of humor would understand. Some sign that he was lying to me.

But there was none.

He simply stared at me, his eyes willing me to believe what he was saying. A dawning sense of horror began to encase me as coldness seeped through my bones. All of the changes I had sensed growing within me. The speed, the growing grace as my inherent clumsiness seemed to fade. The *cravings*. Meat, especially raw meat he'd said. A gurgle, half sob and half hysterical laughter, rushed up my throat as a new realization burst forth.

It wasn't what those creatures had done to me, it wasn't some strange alien germ that had infiltrated my wounds and begun to infect me. Their attacks on me weren't what had brought forth the strange changes I felt coalescing through my body. It had been *him*.

"What did *you* do to me!?" I demanded.

He remained immobile, his eyes didn't even flicker. "The ships started leaking gas into the air supply two weeks prior to The Freezing," he explained instead of telling me what he had done. "The gas was odorless, tasteless, and undetectable to the human race. It's not something your kind had ever heard of before, and to breathe it caused no ill harm unless it was coupled with a high frequency sound that most people can't hear. When the gas and the sound are paired it causes the muscles to freeze, the organs to shut down, and the brain to become suspended. It's something similar to what you would know as cryogenics."

"But cryogenics doesn't work," I mumbled.

"Yet, it doesn't work *yet,* and only because humans haven't mastered it yet."

I felt as if I were trying to wade through a swamp but becoming constantly mired in place by the mud. "Your kind has though."

"Yes. They also designed it so that it wouldn't affect people with type O blood."

My eyes shot back to his, I fought to shake the strange stupor clinging to me. "Why?" I breathed.

"For the hunt, for the thrill, humans are the most dangerous type of game after all. Type O is the most popular blood type, but there wouldn't be enough of the population left to be a serious threat to them, or at least that's what *they* believe. They wanted the hunt, but they also wanted the assurance that they could win. It was decided to leave that number of the population mobile, while being able to easily capture and use the others for food and pleasure. Not everyone will be killed during the reaping process though."

"They'll be left behind for a later time." I was finding it more and more difficult to breathe. The neck of my shirt suddenly felt too tight as it squeezed my windpipe. I slid my finger into it and tugged at it anxiously. I needed to breathe, I couldn't breathe. "For breeding," I choked. "For their children to restock earth, maybe even *my* children." I was never going to have kids; I would *never* allow them to go through this misery. Never let them experience this terror and loss, and I most certainly would *not* lose them to the monsters hunting us now. "No children."

His eyes were sad as he leaned closer to me. "Bethany…"

I shook my head, devastated by what he was telling me. I'd never really thought about children before, I'd assumed that one day I'd have them but they were never a real thought or plan in my life. I was stunned by the sense of loss that filled me. "No."

"You don't have to give that up Bethany. Your dreams…"

"Are changing every day. I'm not even sure I have them anymore Cade, there's no guarantee beyond this moment, this second. I simply want to enjoy every day that I get from here on out. Besides, could we… um is it even possible?" Red crept up my cheeks as my hands closed around his.

"I don't know if conception is possible, but sex is," he answered.

My face was on fire as I managed a small nod. "But if it is, our child, what would it be?"

He shook his head. "There's no way to know Bethany, our breeding period is different than a humans. Our gestation is six months, the labor is not as intense, but our babies are larger. There is no way to know what would happen to you, what it would do to you, and it's not a chance I am willing to take. Not with you." He took a deep breath as something menacing flickered through his eyes. "It doesn't have to be me Bethany."

"No!" I cried, aghast at his words. "Cade that's not what I meant."

"You deserve to have as much of a normal life as you can have under these circumstances. You deserve to have everything that you want in this life."

"No! Stop it Cade! Stop it!" I was infuriated at his words. "I don't want a child Cade, not in this world, not to be hunted, frightened and hungry…"

"It may not always be like that."

Anger flashed hotly through me. "And I most certainly would *not* want another man's child. If we can't have children together then I will not have them. I'm ok with that. I am not ok with this conversation though so please stop, please."

He sighed as he nodded slowly. "If that's what you would like."

Though he said it, I knew he didn't agree with it, or even consider the matter completely dropped as his eyes remained entirely black. I wasn't willing to continue with the conversation, not when there were other more important things to discuss. "Why do you think I'm not completely human? What did you do Cade?"

He took hold of my hands, but they still felt eerily cold within his warm grip. "You're not one of The Frozen Ones because of me." I stared at him, but I was having a difficult time focusing on him. Here was my answer, finally, and I wasn't sure that I wanted to hear it anymore. "Because I was able to change you."

I struggled to see him, struggled to make out the face I loved so much through my suddenly blurred vision. "I don't understand; how is that possible?"

He rubbed his hands over mine as his eyes gradually returned to the eyes I knew so well. "Don't hate me."

I swallowed the lump in my throat. "Cade, what did you do?" I whispered.

"When they told me that they were going to release the gas soon, and who they were going to affect with it, I became determined to find out what your blood type was. I had to know what would become of you and if there was some way that I could stop it. I was able to get a hold of your medical records." I didn't ask how, I was certain he could do anything he put his mind to and for all I knew my doctor was one of them too. "I considered allowing you to freeze and trying to keep you safe after that, but I knew there was no way I could guarantee your safety, or any certainty that I would be able to wake you up again. There was no way to know if they would kill you immediately if I brought you to one of the holding cells. To move you..."

I shook my head at him. I knew how tricky it would have been to move me, to keep me safe in that state. We had lost my mom, and Peter, soon after The Freezing occurred. It had been so difficult to keep my mother alive, so challenging to even get her that far into our journey. I didn't have to hear it from him now, not when I already knew how hard it was.

"There was only one thing I could do, no matter how risky it would be for you, so I gave you some of my blood." My eyes shot up as my mouth dropped. I could only sit there and gape at him dumbfounded. "It was a risk, the biggest risk I've ever taken. My kind has performed many experiments on humans over the centuries and our blood has been given to them in the past. Few have survived."

My insides were curdling up, but they weren't the same insides that I'd been born with. I recalled Bishop's words about my abnormal cells and I had the urge to cry. That hunger, that *craving*. Iron deficiency my ass, I thought derisively.

"I *had* to take the chance that you would survive the infusion of my blood into your system. You wouldn't have kept moving after The Freezing if I didn't. I hoped that my intense reaction to you, and the way that you affected me meant that you were special, that you would be able to handle my blood when most wouldn't. That there was a reason I had met you; that you would survive whatever it did to you. After I gave it to you I monitored you carefully and watched you constantly. I searched for any sign that something might go drastically wrong, but thankfully you seemed to be doing well with it. I didn't know what I was going to do if it went the other way, it wasn't a possibility I would like to consider. If you had died..."

His hands pressed against my face as he leaned even closer. His onyx eyes filled my vision; I could feel his desperate need for my forgiveness, my understanding but I was still too shocked to offer him anything more than numbed silence. "My blood inside of you was how I was able to find you again; it was also how I was able to enter your dream. My blood linked us permanently; I'll always be able to find you anywhere. It's how I found you the day of The Freezing, how I was able to save you."

I felt as if I'd been kicked in the gut at the revelation. I had thought it was just a lucky coincidence that Cade had been near the store that day; instead he'd been following me, preparing to intervene when everything I knew fell apart. The depth of everything I'd never known or suspected was staggering. My head was spinning, my heart lumbered in my chest as I strained to keep a hold on my unraveling composure.

"When did you do this? *How* did you do this?"

"Graduation. I was able to put some of my blood into your drink when you went to the bathroom."

I had been roofied with alien blood at my brother's graduation. I found sick humor in that knowledge. "What happened to the other people that survived?"

Cade grimaced as he closed his eyes. "They began to exhibit differences at a cellular level. They were studied for awhile, but ultimately destroyed when it was determined that the effects were nothing more than abnormal blood cells."

"How long?"

"What?"

I cleared my throat as I grappled to get the words out. "How long were they allowed to live for, and studied, before they were killed?"

"A month, maybe two."

I winced at his words. I'd been alive for almost five months since he had slipped me his blood. More than double the amount of time than any of the others. "Why didn't they keep them alive for longer?"

"They are not good creatures Bethany."

"I know that Cade, believe me I know that. Why?"

"I believe they grew bored with them."

A single tear slid down my face, my head bowed at his words. I knew that he was right about why they had destroyed the people so soon after they had survived the infusion of alien blood. "So there is no way to know if I will become a monster or not?"

"Bethany you will not become a monster."

"You can't know that!" I cried. All of those strange little differences I had noticed in me. So many of them, but the *hunger...* That was the worst, and it was only getting stronger. *What was I? What had he done?* "You can't know what you created! You can't know what I may do tomorrow or the next day or the…"

He grabbed hold of my shoulders. "I know *you*!" he said fiercely. "And no matter what changes this may bring in you, it will *never* change your essence. It will *never* change who *you* are."

I wanted to believe him but there was no way to know for sure what I'd become. Tears filled my eyes; I bit on my bottom lip to keep from crying. *What if I became emotionless and cold? What if I killed someone?* I couldn't imagine drinking blood, or what it would be like to have someone's soul calling out to me.

"I don't want to hurt anyone," I moaned.

"You *won't* Bethany!" he said fervently. "You won't. You don't have that in you, and if there ever comes a day when you might, I'll take you away," he rushed out when I opened my mouth to protest. "I will keep you safe no matter what it takes. I will take care of you no matter what the consequences are if you'll allow me to."

I wanted to tell him everything I was experiencing, but I found that I couldn't. Not now. I was terrified by what was happening to me, but he didn't have to know about it yet. Maybe not ever. He felt bad enough for everything that had happened and didn't need this on top of it. I told myself this, but I knew the real reason was that I was too cowardly to say it out loud. If I did, it would be true. If I uttered the words out loud there would be no more denying what was going on inside of me.

"Abby and Aiden..."

"I will keep them safe also. With my life I will keep you, and everyone that you love, safe. I will not allow you to be destroyed. What I did was selfish, so incredibly selfish and I'm sorry for it, but I simply couldn't stand the thought of living without you. Of having you die in such a way. I didn't know what else to do to keep you safe."

"What if I'd been one of the ones that died?" I wasn't angry that he'd taken this chance with my life without my permission; I would have been dead if he hadn't, or I would have been trapped, frozen in preparation of those hideous things hunting me down. That was a fate worse than death in my opinion.

Blackness momentarily filtered through his eyes again. "I don't know what I would have done; I wouldn't have been able to survive if I'd been the one that destroyed you. I didn't allow myself to think about that consequence. All I thought of was saving you. Please Bethany." His hands were crushing as he pulled me against him. "Please forgive me."

I burst into tears. I was terrified and confused but the distress I heard in his voice was ripping at my insides. How could I tell him that there was something wrong with me, that he may have inadvertently destroyed me, when all he'd intended was to keep me alive and safe? He had sacrificed everything, *everything* for me.

He had gone behind my back, and turned me into something different, but he'd done it because he loved me and I would have done the same if our roles were reversed. I knew that with complete certainty as I clung to him and pulled at him with an intensity that shocked even me. I needed him. I wanted him. I would forever belong to him and be a part of him. He was a part of me, engrained in my cells, bonded with me right down to my DNA.

He'd risked his life to save mine, he was willing to do anything to ensure my happiness, even step aside if I wanted him to. "There's nothing to forgive," I breathed against his warm neck.

"I betrayed you, I…"

"I would have done the same to you, *for* you."

"Bethany."

The way he groaned my name caused shivers to race up and down my spine, my muscles to turn to Jell-O as I became putty in his hands. "That's what Ian meant," I said as realization dawned.

The mention of Ian caused fury to flit briefly over his features. "What he meant when?" he grated.

"When he said to me, 'He's inside of you. You smell and taste like him you know.' I hadn't understood it at the time, but he must have somehow sensed your blood inside of me. Perhaps when he drank it, or when he tried to get inside of me with that…"

"What!?" Cade snarled. I recoiled as black filled his eyes. I didn't know if it was the fact that he was so enraged, or the fact that I now knew the truth, but for the first time his control slipped completely as lines of black zigzagged rapidly across his face and down his neck.

"It came out of him, it oozed…" I stuttered out. "It didn't hurt as bad as when that creature tore into my shoulder, but…" Cade swore violently as he released me. He launched to his feet and stormed around the forest. His hands fisted, the muscles in his arms stood starkly out against his skin. I drew my legs against my chest as the blackness began to seep down his neck. It wasn't him that I was afraid of, he would never harm me, but his reaction to what Ian had done terrified me. "Cade, you're scaring me. What did he do?"

I barely recognized him as he spun toward me. It seemed as if the devil himself was seeping throughout Cade's body, highlighting every vein as even his arms began to turn black. I imagined it ran all the way down his chest as well. Perhaps it even started at his heart and pulsed out with every beat instead of originating at his eyes, like I'd first thought.

He took a step toward me and suddenly I understood where so many horror legends had been born. Vampires, succubae, demons, of course evil aliens, and probably a host of other monsters that had been created over the centuries had all gotten their start here, in Cade's face, in his eyes, in his *heritage*. Those myths had been created by people who had been terrified to see this same exact visage. Who had witnessed one of these creatures drinking from a human, who had seen the black cloud that Ian had emitted, and the blackness that engulfed Cade. The stories had been twisted and recreate in one way or another. There were no vampire teeth, succubae were not all women, and demons didn't come from the depths of Hell. At least I didn't think they did as I was fairly certain now that all those legends had originated from the sky.

Cade's face gradually returned to normal but his eyes remained a solid black. He came back to kneel before me. The whites of his eyes became apparent again as he clasped hold of me. His hands were on my face once more, stroking and demanding as he tilted my face to his. "How *long* was he inside of you Bethany?"

I shook my head as I bit on my bottom lip. "It seemed like forever, it hurt…" I broke off as his face flooded once more. "I don't think it was very long," I blurted.

I didn't dare tell him I had nearly passed out from it; he already seemed on the verge of snapping once more without that added detail. His eyes searched mine as he leaned closer to me. "I don't think he took much."

I shuddered, not at all liking that statement. I didn't like to think about Ian taking *anything* from me. Something passed over Cade's features as his hands clenched on mine. "What if he did, how would I know? What would it do to me?"

He shook his head. "Less of a soul, perhaps a little less human."

"I'm *already* less human! I can't be any less than that Cade, I simply can't!"

"I'm sure that you're fine Bethany. I would see the difference already, I would *feel* it. He would have planned to draw out the torture, to extend it for as long as possible. In order to do so he wouldn't take much from you."

"So he said," I muttered bitterly. "He wanted to punish me, but mostly he wanted to punish *you*."

Despair twisted his features. "I promise you that no one will *ever* touch you like that again." I tried to find solace in his words, but I was terrified, and I was suddenly very cold. "Let's get you out of here. You're freezing."

He helped me to my feet, but it was not the chilly air that was causing my shivers to increase. It was the ice that encompassed my bones and my soul. Even now there may be something growing inside of me, twisting me, changing me into someone that I may not know. I couldn't even trust my own body anymore. I tilted my head back to look up at his locked jaw; his gaze remained focused ahead as he led me through the forest.

He was nearly perfect, but that beauty hid something sinister and deadly that I'd never suspected could reside beneath that magnificent exterior, something that *only* cared about me. Abby had told me once that I was the only one Cade warmed to; I had wanted to tell her she was wrong that he wasn't as cold as he appeared, but I'd never lied to my sister and I hadn't then. She'd been right, I'd known it, but I hadn't truly gotten it until now.

The only thing human about Cade was *me*.

Without me he was just as harsh, brutal, and volatile as the rest of his kind, a fact that he had proven with his unremorseful slaughter of Ian. The good in him was *really* good, but the viciousness within him was just as engrained and encompassing. I shuddered to think what he would become, what he would *do* if something ever happened to me. It would be horrible.

"Can they be defeated?"

His shoulders slumped as he shook his head. "I don't know Bethany. The way we stand now, no. If we could find a larger group of survivors we may be able to put up a bigger fight, but I'm not sure if that's going to happen. For now, it's probably best if we lay low and try to survive until we find a safer place to stay. They normally don't stay in one place too long as they tend to get bored. The other planets they've taken over did not possess any human-like intelligence." He turned to me and his eyes leisurely scanned over me. "Or your powerful survival instinct. They've known all along that humans would be their biggest challenge."

"Good," I replied forcefully. They may be kicking our asses, but I took pride in the fact that they were also concerned about us. They'd had to decimate our population in order to cripple us as badly as they had. "What are those creatures that are hunting us Cade? Are they like you? Are they pets? What *are* they?"

He draped his arm around my shoulder and pulled me against his side. "They were genetically engineered for another planet, one that my kind couldn't survive on due to the air being inhospitable for them to breathe. They were set loose to collect blood and bring back survivors in order to harvest the souls. It wasn't until Earth, and the large population it possessed, that the victims were frozen first to keep the resistance down. An ingredient to wake the people was added to the creatures."

"Why did they do that though? Why do they reawaken them?"

"Because they enjoy the suffering."

"Of course they do," I muttered bitterly.

"It is only *extreme* agony that will wake people from The Freezing, only those things. It's why I never told you about it, why I never tried to have your mother reawakened."

"I would have lost her either way."

He pulled my closer against him and kissed the top of my head. "I'm sorry Bethany, if there was something I could have done…"

"It's ok, I know. She never had to know that kind of pain thankfully. Was she aware of her death?" I had to force the words out of me, I'd asked the question but I wasn't sure I wanted the answer.

"No, they aren't aware of what is happening to them." Relief filled me as I slumped against him. She hadn't suffered, she hadn't known. It was more solace than I'd ever hoped to find in the senseless and malicious death of my mother. "The brain is immobilized also. I'm sure if there was a way for them to figure out how to shut everything down, and keep the brain running they would, but thankfully they haven't conquered that bit of cruelty yet."

I shuddered at the thought. "Thankfully."

"It is a new technology, one that they haven't mastered yet, but they planned to make sure that their creatures, or pets if you will, were at the very least able to reawaken the humans and they wanted to make sure they suffered in the awakening. They also had to make sure that the humans that were awakened again were kept immobile until they could be brought to a holding area."

"And that pain definitely keeps someone immobile."

His fingers stroked over my arm. "I wish I could take that from you."

I brushed back a loose strand of hair. "I'm glad I know, I suppose." It wasn't something I was happy to be stuck with but I was glad I knew what those other people were going through. "You knew that when you burned Peter though."

"I didn't burn Peter; he wasn't a bad old man I wouldn't harm him for no reason."

"But I smelled hair…"

"I heal fast." My eyebrows shot into my hairline as I gaped at him. He hadn't harmed Peter after all, maybe there was a little more human in him than I'd thought.

"Those things don't drain the soul?"

"No, that's only us."

"Have they always been able to mimic a human being?"

I didn't like the stormy look that crossed his face. "That is a new talent," he said slowly. "One that I didn't even know about, but the leaders don't share all of their secrets, especially not with the ones of us that have been put on Earth."

"Why not?"

He shrugged absently. "We're not privy to the inner circle, not once we're placed here. Our main duties are to infiltrate and report our findings. The politics that play out amongst the leaders have little impact on our lives. I was only told when the invasion was going to happen a month before graduation."

"I see." I frowned as I thought over his words. "If this hadn't happened, you never would have come for me, would you? You would have let me stay with Bret."

His eyes closed as he folded his arms over his chest. "I hated you with him, I truly did, but yes I would have left you alone to live your own life. If I thought they would have allowed me to be with you, to marry you, I would have come for you in a heartbeat. However, though we do not have children with them, we are only allowed to marry influential and powerful people, if we marry humans at all. It had already been established that I would marry one of my kind; she had been adopted by a couple that possessed old money and lots of power. It was a match that was made as soon as I was placed with the Marshall's, we were going to meet at college and marry after graduation. I've never met her."

My fingers clenched on the rigid muscles of his abdomen as I took a deep breath in order to remain calm. He was so cold, so analytical about marrying a girl he'd never even known, and he would have done it, I was certain of that. "If I'd ever even hinted that I wanted to marry you, to be with you, they would have killed you. If I'd tried to deny the arrangement they would have killed me."

"You would have married her."

"And I would have known where you were every minute of my life. When they decided to invade I still would have come for you. I would have taken you, Bret, your children..."

"Cade..."

"And I would have saved you *all* if it would have made you happy Bethany. It would have destroyed me to let another man have you but I never would have put your life in jeopardy."

"You could have come to me, you could have explained," I breathed. "I would have listened to you, I would have believed you; I would have run away with you."

"And left your family behind?" I opened my mouth to say yes, but the word froze in my throat. "They had already known the loss of your father; would you have left them still?"

"I would have loved you."

A single strand of midnight hair fell into the corner of his eye as he tilted his head to look at me. "I know you would have, and it would have gotten you nothing but a life of secrets and misery. It may have even cost you your life. I wasn't going to let that happen, no matter how badly I wanted to be with you."

My heart swelled with love for him as tears slid down my face. "What do *you* take your souls from?"

"Animals mostly, but when it's been absolutely necessary I have taken from a person without their knowledge. Not you," he reminded me forcefully when my head shot toward him. "I never take too much, but sometimes the craving is too strong for just an animal to satisfy me. It's rare that happens though, maybe twice a year, sometimes three. It's the blood we need more than the soul. That's at least once a week, preferably more, and since all of this started my appetite has been even more intense and demanding."

It was disconcerting but not awful, I decided. The ice in his eyes thawed as he looked down at me. "It's more difficult when I'm around, isn't it?"

"Not so much harder." He grated out. "I just want you more than I've ever wanted anything." I was frightened and yet strangely enthralled by his words. "Nothing will satisfy me the way that I know you would."

My mouth parted, my heart hammered as my toes curled and my body spun with the longing to touch and feel and know *more* of him. What did that say about me? What normal person would actually crave for someone to feed off of their soul, off of their blood? I was disconcerted by the implications of my intense need for him to touch me in such a way. "You could…"

"No," he interrupted briskly as his face returned to that blank mask I was beginning to despise. "That cannot happen. I won't take the chance of possibly hurting you."

"You're amazing to deny yourself even when I'm offering myself freely to you."

"Am I?" he inquired with wry amusement.

"Yes."

"Careful love, you shouldn't flatter the devil too much."

I started at the reminder of what the girls in school had called him, the black devil. They hadn't known just how spot on they'd been with that description. *Perhaps that's the way another legend had been born,* I realized. I imagined that these invaders must have resembled the devil when they had arrived to decimate populations.

"What are we going to tell the others about Ian?"

"I'll take care of it." His eyes raked the marks on my neck. "I'll have to find you a shirt that hides those marks first though. I'm sure they've already looked for you in your room."

I nodded as I bit on my bottom lip. I trusted that he would be able to handle it, but I was an awful liar, and Aiden had always been able to read me like a book.

CHAPTER 18

A week later Aiden was still staring at me questioningly and watching me like a hawk. I tried to ignore his scrutiny, but it was becoming increasingly more difficult to do so. Everyone seemed wary of everyone else within the group, but I was certain that Aiden knew I was lying about sneaking out to be with Cade at the time that Ian had been killed. Certain that he suspected Cade as his gaze slid toward Cade and Aiden inspected him with the same distrust I'd seen grow over the past week.

The decision to leave the hotel immediately had been made before the two of us had even returned to the hotel. We came back to find our stuff waiting for us and Aiden, Bret, and Lloyd preparing to set off in search of us. Darnell and Bishop had just finished burying Ian's broken body. I hadn't had to fake the blush that stained my cheeks when Aiden confronted us. The turtleneck Cade had managed to smuggle from the hotel helped with our story, even if it actually wasn't hiding hickeys beneath the high collar. It couldn't hide the bruises on my face though, but they had been explained away by training, and a clumsy accident with a tree branch.

That explanation hadn't been bought, at least not by Aiden, and I suspected some of the others.

Bishop was still openly mourning the loss of his equipment, data, and fresh samples of my tainted blood. I didn't know how I was going to tell him that he couldn't take anymore of my blood, but I decided to cross that bridge when we came to it, if we ever came to it. I hoped Cade had formulated some kind of plan, but we hadn't discussed it, and I didn't really want to. Not yet anyway.

Ian's death had been attributed to the fact that he must have interrupted someone in the act of stealing the supplies, or vandalizing them. Some had bought the explanation, others hadn't. The group was disjointed and not as close anymore. They tried to believe that it had been someone outside of the group that had killed Ian, but the doubt was obviously festering. A few more people had decided that they would be better off on their own. I longed to tell them that they were safe, that even though the killer *was* still amongst us, he wouldn't hurt them, but I couldn't do that without betraying Cade's trust. Instead I stood motionless, desolate, and guilty as they disappeared into the forest. Cade held my hand, his solid strength helping me to get through the sadness that encompassed me.

We hadn't settled into any one area for more than enough time to sleep since we'd left the hotel behind. The days were becoming colder and shorter, October first rolled around as we reached the outskirts of Boston. For months the large alien ship had hovered over the city, but on the day of The Freezing it had moved over the ocean. Cade had explained it was a safety measure because there weren't as many on the ship now that they were needed to guard over their prisoners, and to take pleasure in hunting down the less fortunate. They didn't think us much of a threat anymore, especially since they'd managed to disarm so many before The Freezing had occurred, but they still weren't going to take any unnecessary risks with their ship.

A cornered animal was the most treacherous, and we were certainly cornered. I was determined to show them just how dangerous and deadly we could be, but there were other things we had to do first. Jenna's family was still out there, we were in need of food and ammo, but most of all we *had* to find more survivors. There was strength in numbers, and we had to increase ours, instead of having them steadily decrease.

We stood on a hill overlooking the abandoned stretches of highway and bridges that crisscrossed into the heart of Boston. The once proud city looked desolate and terrifying. I had been here only once before, when I was a child on our last family trip together. We'd gone to the aquarium and science museum. I'd been fascinated by the tall buildings, the traffic, and the people. My father had taken Aiden and I by Fenway Park and proudly spouted the history of the Sox, and The Curse. He hadn't survived to see them break it.

I searched the empty roads, the broken buildings, and debris for any signs of life. It had once been a city of nearly three quarters of a million. There was no sign that *any* of those people still lived. But there had to be survivors, there simply *had* to be people amongst the skyscrapers, warehouses, broken concrete, and shattered glass. I expected to see wild animals creeping through the twisted byways, reclaiming the land they'd lost, but there was no movement on the littered asphalt. There was a hushed, peculiar pall hanging over the city. None of us seemed willing to break the silence, or even move, as we stared in awe at the ruined remnants of a once glorious world that had ceased to exist.

There were a handful of cars on the roads, a sight that was surprising and unnerving. Vehicles had been banned before The Freezing had occurred, it was the first time I'd seen any on the road in months. Some people must have panicked and tried to drive into the city after The Freezing. I didn't know what had become of those people, but I suspected they hadn't made it far. There was no way that they could have as they would have been sitting ducks on the roadways.

"We'll make camp here." Darnell's voice was hoarse with emotion. "From now on we'll travel at night as the concrete jungle won't hide us the same as the woods."

It didn't seem like much of a jungle to me anymore.

I glanced at the group gathered around us; our numbers had dwindled to only nineteen, a far cry from the nearly sixty that had been in the warehouse over a month ago. It was still a lot of people to move through these streets, but if we were careful we could make it without losing any more. We would just have to stay in the shelter of the buildings and alleyways. I turned away from the city, frightened and nervous by what was to come.

I looked to Jenna. She was wringing her hands as her eyes searched the city below us. Darnell had promised her that we would try to get to as many of the addresses on her list as possible, but there was no guarantee it could be done. I couldn't even begin to imagine what she was going through. I didn't like the answers I had, but at least I *knew* what had become of my mother.

Abby grabbed hold of Jenna's arm and squeezed it as she sought to give Jenna some comfort. I wrapped my arm around her as I settled against the trunk of a large maple. The leaves hadn't started to change color yet but they would soon. We would have to be away from the city, and somewhere secure, before the woods became bare and winter set in. We didn't have much time to spare looking for survivors, or more medicinal supplies. The mission was supposed to be a quick in and out affair in which we gathered as many supplies as possible.

I hoped that it worked that way, but I had come to learn that nothing ever went as planned anymore.

Cade settled down on the other side of me. He draped his arm around my shoulders and pulled me against his side. I closed my eyes as I lost myself to the reassuring beat of his heart. His warmth enveloped me in a cocoon of security. Abby snuggled closer to me, her head rested against my shoulder as her breathing evened out and her body relaxed. Barney yawned as he settled in beside her and rested his head in her lap. A moment of solace enveloped me as the warmth and love of my family enveloped me.

Cade would keep us safe, I thought sleepily. His hand moved idly through my hair, he twirled it around his finger as his lips rested briefly on the back of my neck. I shivered before lifting my head and smiling at him. His ebony eyes gleamed with warmth and love as his fingers played over my cheek.

I turned my attention away from him before I became lost to the emotions he aroused in me. Aiden was staring at us with narrowed eyes. Cade shifted beside me, his hand pulled me closer as he spotted Aiden. I wondered how long it would be before my brother confronted me, I was amazed he had waited this long.

Suddenly Bret was before us. He knelt down and handed me a plate of beans, beef jerky, and a piece of bread. "I know you hate jerky, but we're running low on food."

"It's fine, thanks." I smiled at him as I took my plate. At least it was meat. I shifted uncomfortably, hating that realization, but it was true. Cade's hand slipped off my shoulders as he accepted his meager lunch also. Abby didn't stir but I took her food and placed it beside her for later.

"Make sure you eat it. It's going to be a long night," Bret told me.

I nodded and Bret rose and walked away swiftly. I forced the dry jerky down my throat, choosing to eat it first in order to get it out of the way. This was not the time to be picky about food; I doubted I would ever have that luxury again. I choked down the last swallow before eagerly digging into the cold baked beans that remained.

I tried to sleep before night settled in, but I was wound so tight that I found it nearly impossible to do so. Once we hit the city our pace would be far more frantic and rushed. None of us wanted to stay there for any longer than we had to. I only hoped that everyone would be able to keep up with the harsh pace that Darnell had described.

Eventually I was able to drift off, but it felt as if I had barely closed my eyes before Cade was shaking me awake again. "It's time," he whispered in my ear.

I nodded, swallowed heavily and rose to my feet. I joined the others at the top of the hill and gazed down at the now gloomy ribbons of highway. One of the cars had its lights on; it must have had an automatic nighttime sensor. Though the battery was dying, its dim glow was enough to illuminate ten feet in front of the car, giving the road an eerie radiance that caused the hair on the nape of my neck to stand up.

 Darnell jerked his head to the side to signal for Mick to take the lead. We moved rapidly forward, staying low as we took the hill as carefully, and rapidly, as possible. The city was a whole new world than the one we had been living in, and I was terrified of everything it hid within its concrete depths. There was no way of knowing what Boston had in store for us.

 No way of knowing what was to come of this leg of our journey, but I couldn't shake the feeling that hidden within these high walls, ominous roadways, and numerous hiding spots were far more threats than we had already encountered.

Where to find the author

Webpage: https://ericastevensauthor.com/home.html

Facebook: https://www.facebook.com/#!/ericastevens679

Blog: http://ericasteven.blogspot.com/

Twitter: @EricaStevensCGP

Mailing list: ericastevensgcp@gmail.com

About the author

My name is not really Erica Stevens, it is a pen name that I chose in memory of two amazing friends lost to soon. However, I was born in New York and moved to Mass as a child. I spent my time growing up between NY and Mass so I have some interesting times when sports games roll around. I was fortunate enough to marry my best friend and I don't know what I'd do without him. We share our home with our crazy dog Loki and fish Klinger. I have a large, crazy, fun loving family that just loves to laugh. My parents, siblings, nieces and nephews have taught me a lot and made my life much more entertaining and enjoyable. I love to read and have wanted to be a writer ever since I was a child.

Printed in Great Britain
by Amazon.co.uk, Ltd.,
Marston Gate.